LAW OF THE
DESERT BORN

LAW OF THE DESERT BORN

Louis L'Amour

CARROLL & GRAF PUBLISHERS, INC.

New York

First Carroll & Graf edition 1983

ISBN: 0-671-06697-8

Carroll & Graf Publishers, Inc.
260 Fifth Avenue
New York, N.Y. 10001

Printed in the United States of America

Contents

LAW OF THE
DESERT BORN

FOREWORD

The stories included in this volume originally appeared a number of years ago. One story, "The Black Rock Coffin-Makers" was first published under the pen name "Jim Mayo." Another story, "Trap of Gold" was reprinted in a collection entitled, *War Party*. This edition is a first to present these vintage Louis L'Amour works in one collection.

Louis L'Amour is part of the tradition of American Western fiction that has its roots in The Leather-Stocking Tales of James Fenimore Cooper and grew with America's expansion westward, reaching its fervor in the building of the transcontinental railroad—a monumental task that captivated the American imagination.

The Civil War played a major role in establishing the "western" as a distinct and highly commercial genre. The "dime novel" came into its own in the 1860's with the outbreak of the Civil War, serving as a means of cheap entertainment for the soldiers, as the comic book did for the inductees in the bootcamps of World War II.

Cooper's Natty Bumpo was transfigured into the likes of "Deadeye Dick" and "Sierra Sam" and culminated in the much heralded "Buffalo Bill" whose exploits were penned by Edward Zane Carroll Judson, world renowned as "Ned Buntline," and later by the impressive and prolific Colonel Prentiss Ingraham. In 1896, Street & Smith, the leading publisher of dime novels, began collecting the serials into small papercovered books thus giving birth to the mass market paperback.

Frank A. Munsey launched the pulp magazine in 1896 by creating a new format for *Argosy* with the use of cheap pulp paper. This masterstroke of publishing ingenuity provided a new forum for the Western and, with the addition of the legendary Robert H. Davis as editorial director of The Frank A. Munsey, Company, the Western reached new heights. During his tenure at the helm of the Munsey magazine empire, Bob Davis made two major discoveries for Western fiction: Zane Grey and Frederick Schiller Faust (best known as simply "Max Brand"). These two authors grew rapidly in reputation and soon came to the attention of the editors at Street & Smith, then firmly entrenched in the pulp magazine field and Munsey's arch-rivals.

At Street & Smith, Zane Grey matured in his craft under the astute direction and reassuring guidance of the brilliant Charles Agnew MacLean.

In 1919, Street & Smith premiered *Western Story Magazine*, the very first pulp magazine specializing in the genre. Its pages were filled with all the top names of the day including George Owen Baxter, David Manning, Evin Evans, all of whom were none other than the *noms de plume* of Frederick S. Faust.

Western Story Magazine lorded supreme over all the other Western pulps until December 1932, when Popular Publications debuted *Dime Western Magazine*, which then became "The Leading Western Magazine" with its new, livelier approach to the western. Popular Publications soon followed with *Star Western* which also built a tremendous following and featured the early works of Frederick D. Glidden writing as "Luke Short."

The publication of *Shane* by Jack Schaefer in the pages of *Argosy* in 1946 under the title "Rider from Nowhere" marked the beginning of the end of the pulps, for *Argosy* had by then gone slick and the age of the modern paperback was at hand. Ten years later, the pulps had all but vanished.

Louis L'Amour served his apprenticeship as a writer in the pulps and became a journeyman, then master while writing for the paperbacks. The stories collected in this edition reflect that bygone era of sensation when the reader could smell the heady scents of gunpowder, leather and pulp.

THE PUBLISHERS

LAW OF THE
DESERT BORN

Shad Marone crawled out of the water swearing, and slid into the mesquite. Suddenly, for the first time since the chase began, he was mad. He was mad clear through. "The hell with it!" He got to his feet, his eyes blazing. "I've run far enough! If they cross Black River, they're askin' for it!"

For three days he had been on the dodge, using every strategem known to men of the desert, but they clung to him like leeches. That was what came of killing a sheriff's brother, and the fact that he killed in self-defense wasn't going to help a bit. Especially when the killer was Shad Marone.

That was what you could expect when you were the last man of the losing side in a cattle war. All his friends were gone now but Madge.

The best people of Puerto de Luna hadn't been the toughest in this scrap, and they had lost. And Shad Marone, who had been one of the toughest, had lost with them. His guns hadn't been enough to outweigh those of the other faction.

Of course, he admitted to himself, those on his side hadn't been angels. He'd branded a few head of calves himself from time to time, and when cash was short he had often run a few steers over the border. But hadn't they all?

Truman and Dykes had been good men, but Dykes had been killed at the start, and Truman had fought like a gentleman, and that wasn't any way to win in the Black River country.

Since then, there had been few peaceful days for Shad Marone.

After they'd elected Clyde Bowman sheriff, he knew they were out to get him. Bowman hated him, and Bowman had been one of the worst of them in the cattle war.

The trouble was, Shad was a gun fighter and they all knew it. Bowman was fast with a gun, and in a fight could hold his own. Also, he was smart enough to leave Shad Marone strictly alone. So they just waited, watched, and planned.

Shad had taken their dislike as a matter of course. It took tough men to settle a tough country, and if they started shooting, somebody got hurt. Well, he wasn't getting hurt. There had been too much shooting to suit him.

He wanted to leave Puerto de Luna, but Madge

was still living on the old place, and he didn't
want to leave her there alone. So he stayed on,
knowing it couldn't last.

Then Jud Bowman rode into town. Shad was
thoughtful when he heard that. Jud was notori-
ously quarrelsome, and was said to have twelve
notches on his gun. Shad had a feeling that Jud
hadn't come to Puerto de Luna by accident.

Jud hadn't been in town two days before the
grapevine had the story that if Clyde and Lopez
were afraid to run Marone out of town, he wasn't.

Jud Bowman might have done it too, if it hadn't
been for Tips. Tips Hogan had been tending bar in
Puerto de Luna for a long time. He'd come over
the trail as wagon boss for Shad's old man, something everyone had forgotten but Shad and Tips
himself.

Tips saw the gun in Bowman's lap, and he gave
Marone a warning. It was just a word, through
unmoving lips, while he mopped the bar.

After a moment, Shad turned, his glass in his
left hand, and he saw the way Bowman was sitting,
and how the table top would conceal a gun in his
lap. Even then, when he knew they had set things
up to kill him, he hadn't wanted trouble. He decided to get out while the getting was good. Then
he saw Slade near the door and Henderson across
the room.

He was boxed. They weren't gambling this time.
Tips Hogan knew what was coming, and he was
working his way down the bar.

Marone took it easy. He knew it was coming, and it wasn't a new thing. That was his biggest advantage, he thought. He had been in more tights than any of them. He didn't want any more trouble, but if he got out of this it would be right behind a sixgun. The back door was barred and the window closed.

Jud Bowman looked up suddenly. He had a great shock of blonde, coarse hair, and under bushy brows his eyes glinted. "What's this about you threatenin' to kill me, Marone?"

So that was their excuse. He had not threatened Bowman, scarcely knew him, in fact, but this was the way to put him in wrong, to give them the plea of self-defense.

He let his eyes turn to Bowman, saw the tensity in the man's face. A denial, and there would be shooting. Jud's right hand finger tips rested on the table's edge. He had only to drop a hand and fire.

"Huh?" Shad said stupidly, as though startled from a day dream. He took a step toward the table, his face puzzled. "Wha'd you say? I didn't get it."

They had planned it all very carefully. Marone would deny, Bowman would claim he'd been called a liar, there would be a killing. They were tense, all three of them set to draw.

"Huh?" Shad repeated, blankly.

They were caught flat-footed. After all, you couldn't shoot a man in cold blood. You couldn't shoot a man who was half asleep. Most of the men in the saloon were against Marone, but they would never stand for murder.

They were poised for action, and nothing happened. Shad blinked at them. "Sorry," he said, "I must've been dreamin'. I didn't hear you."

Bowman glanced around uncertainly wetting his lips with his tongue. "I said I heard you threatened to kill me," he repeated. It sounded lame, and he knew it, but Shad's response had been unexpected. What happened then was even more unexpected.

Marone's left hand shot out and before anyone could move, the table was spun from in front of Bowman. Everyone saw the naked gun lying in his lap.

Every man in the saloon knew that Jud Bowman, for all his reputation, had been afraid to shoot it out with an even break. It would have been murder.

Taken by surprise, Bowman blinked foolishly. Then his wits came back. Blood rushed to his face. He grabbed the gun. "Why, you . . . !"

Then Shad Marone shot him. Shad shot him through the belly, and before the other two could act, he wheeled, not toward the door, but to the closed window. He battered it with his shoulder and went right on through. Outside, he hit the ground on his hands, but came up in a lunging run. Then he was in the saddle and on his way.

There were men in the saloon who would tell the truth—two at least, although neither had much use for him. But Marone knew that with Clyde Bowman as sheriff he would never be brought to trial. He would be killed "evading arrest."

For three days he fled, and during that time they were never more than an hour behind him. Then, at Forked Tree, they closed in. He got away, but they clipped his horse. The roan stayed on his feet, giving all he had, as horses always had given for Shad Marone, and then died on the river bank, still trying with his last breath.

Marone took time to cache his saddle and bridle, then started on afoot. He made the river, and they thought that would stop him, for he couldn't swim a stroke. But he found a drift log, and with his guns riding high, he shoved off. Using the current and his own kicking, he got to the other bank, considerably downstream.

The thing that bothered him was the way they clung to his trail. Bowman wasn't the man to follow as little trail as he left. Yet the man hung to him like an Apache.

Apache!

Why hadn't he thought of that? It would be Lopez, following that trail, not Bowman. Bowman was a bulldog, but Lopez was wily as a fox and bloodthirsty as a weasel.

Shad got to his feet and shook the water from him like a dog. He was a big, rawboned, sunbrowned man. His shirt was half torn away, and a bandolier of cartridges was slung across his shoulder and chest. His sixgun was on his hip, his rifle in his hand.

He poured the water out of his boots. Well, he was through playing now. If they wanted a trail, he'd see that they got one.

Lopez was the one who worried him. He could shake the others, but Lopez was one of the men who had built this country. He was ugly, he killed freely and often, he was absolutely ruthless, but he had nerve. You had to hand it to him. The man wasn't honest, and he was too quick to kill, but it had taken men like him to tame this wild, lonely land. It was a land that didn't tame easy.

Well, what they'd get now would be death for them all. Even Lopez. This was something he'd been saving.

Grimly he turned up the steep, little used path from the river. They thought they had him at the river. And they would think they had him again at the lava beds.

Waterless, treeless and desolate, the lava beds were believed to harbor no life of any kind. Only sand, and great, jagged rocks—rocks shaped like flame—grotesque, barren, awful. More than seventy miles long, never less than thirty miles wide, and so rough a pair of shoes wouldn't last five miles and footing next to impossible for horses.

On the edge of the lava, Shad Marone sat down and pulled off his boots. Tying their strings, he hung them to his belt. Then he pulled out a pair of moccasins he always carried, and slipped them on.

Pliable and easy on his feet, they would give to the rough rock, and would last many times as long in this terrain as boots. He got up and walked into the lava beds.

The bare lava caught the fierce heat and threw it back in his face. A trickle of sweat started down his cheek. He knew the desert, knew how to live in the heat, and he did not try to hurry. That would be fatal. Far ahead of him was a massive tower of rock, jutting up like a church steeple from a tiny village. He headed that way, walking steadily. He made no attempt to cover his trail, no attempt to lose his pursuers. He knew where he was going.

An hour passed, and then another. It was slow going. The rock tower had come abreast of him and then fallen behind. Once he saw the trail of some tiny creature, perhaps a horned frog.

Once, when he climbed a steep declivity, he glanced back. They were still coming. They hadn't quit.

Lopez: That was like Lopez. He wouldn't quit. Shad smiled then, but his eyes were without humor. All right, they wanted to kill him bad enough to try the lava beds. They would have to learn the hard way—learn when they could never profit from the lesson.

He kept working north, using the shade carefully. There was little of it, only here and there in the lee of a rock. But each time he stopped, he cooled off a little. So far he hadn't taken a drink.

After the third hour he washed his lips and rinsed his mouth. Twice, after that, he took only a spoonful of water and rinsed his mouth before swallowing.

Occasionally he stopped and looked around to get his bearings. He smiled grimly when he thought of Bowman. The sheriff was a heavy man. Davis would be there, too. Lopez was lean and wiry. He would last. He would be hard to kill.

By his last count there were eight left. Four had turned back at the lava beds. He gained a little.

At three in the afternoon he finally stopped. It was a nice piece of shade, and would grow better as the hours went on. The ground was low, and in one corner there was a pocket. He dug with his hands until the ground became damp. Then he lay back on the sand and went to sleep.

He wasn't worried. Too many years he had been awakening at the hour he wished, his senses alert to danger. He was an hour ahead of them, at least. He would need this rest he was going to get. What lay ahead would take everything he had. He knew that.

Their feet would be punishing them cruelly now. Three of them still had their horses, leading them.

He rested his full hour, then got up. He had cut it very thin. Through a space in the rocks he could see them, not three hundred yards away. Lopez, as he had suspected, was in the lead. How easy to pick them off now! But no, he would not kill again. Let their own anxiety to kill him kill them.

Within a hundred yards he had put two jumbled piles of boulders between himself and his pursuers. A little farther then, and he stopped.

Before him was a steep slide of shale, near the edge of a great basin. Standing where he did, he could see far away in the distance, a purple haze over the mountains. Between there was nothing but a great white expanse, shimmering with heat.

He slid down the shale and brought up at the bottom. He was now, he knew, seventy feet below sea level. He started away, and at every step dry, powdery dust lifted in clouds. It caked in his nostrils, filmed his eyelashes, and covered his clothes with whitish, alkaline dust. Far across the Sink, and scarcely discernible from the crest behind him, was the Window in the Rock. He headed for it, walking steadily. It was ten miles if you walked straight across.

"So far that Navajo was right," Shad told himself. "An' he said to make it before dark . . . or else!"

Shad Marone's lips were dry and cracked. After a mile he stopped, tilting his canteen until he could get his finger into the water, then carefully moistened his lips. Just a drop then, inside his mouth.

All these men were desertwise. None of them, excepting perhaps Lopez, would know about the Sink. They would need water. They would have to know where to find it. By day they could follow his trail, but after darkness fell . . . ?

And then, the Navajo had said, the wind would

begin to blow. Shad looked at the dry, powdery stuff under him. He could imagine what a smothering, stifling horror this would be if the wind blew. Then, no man could live.

Heat waves danced a queer rigadoon across the lower sky, and heat lifted, beating against his face from the hot white dust beneath his feet. Always it was over a man's shoe tops, sometimes almost knee deep. Far away the mountains were a purple line that seemed to waver vaguely in the afternoon sun. He walked on, heading by instinct rather than sight for the Window.

Dust arose in a slow, choking cloud. It came up from his feet in little puffs, like white smoke. He stumbled, then got his feet right, and kept on. Walking in this was like dragging yourself through heavy mud. The dust pulled at his feet. His pace was slow.

Thirst gathered in his throat, and his mouth seemed filled with something thick and clotted. His tongue was swollen, his lips cracked and swollen. He could not seem to swallow.

He could not make three miles an hour. Darkness would reach him before he made the other side. But he would be close. Close enough. Luckily, at this season, the light stayed long in the sky.

After a long time, he stopped and looked back. Yes, they were coming. But there was not one dust cloud. There were several. Through red-rimmed, sun-squinted eyes, he watched. They were straggling. Every straggler would die. He knew that. Well, they had asked for it.

Dust covered his clothing, and only his gun he kept clean. Every half hour he stopped and wiped it as clean as he could. Twice he pulled a knotted string through the barrel.

Finally he used the last of his water. Every half hour he had been wetting his lips. He did not throw the canteen away, but slung it back upon his hip. He would need it, later, when he got to the Nest. His feet felt very heavy, his legs seemed to belong to an automaton. Head down, he slogged wearily on. In an hour he made two miles.

There is a time when human nature seems able to stand no more. There is a time when every iota of strength seems burned away. This was the fourth day of the chase. Four days without a hot meal, four days of riding, walking, running. Now this. He had only to stop, they would come up with him, and it would be over.

The thought of how easy it would be to quit came to him. He considered the thought. But he did not consider quitting. He could no more have stopped than a bee could stop making honey. Life was ahead, and he had to live. It was a matter only of survival now. The man with the greatest urge to live would be the one to survive.

Those men behind him were going to die. They were going to die for three reasons. First, he alone knew where there was water, and at the right time he would lose them.

Second, he was in the lead, and after dark they would have no trail, and if they lived through the night there would be no trail left in the morning.

Third, at night, at this season, the wind always blew, and their eyes and mouths and ears would fill with soft, white filmy dust, and if they lay down, they would be buried by the sifting, swirling dust.

They would die then, every man jack of them.

They had it coming. Bowman deserved it, so did Davis and Gardner. Lopez most of all. They were all there, he had seen them. Lopez was a killer. The man's father had been Spanish and Irish, his mother an Apache.

Without Lopez he would have shaken them off long ago. Shad Marone tried to laugh, but the sound was only a choking grunt. Well, they had followed Lopez to their death, all of them. Aside from Lopez, they were weak sisters.

He looked back again. He was gaining on them now. The first dust cloud was farther behind, and the distance between the others was growing wider. It was a shame Lopez had to die, at that. The man was tough and had plenty of trail savvy.

Shad Marone moved on. From somewhere within him he called forth a new burst of strength. His eyes watched the sun. While there was light, they had a chance. What would they think in Puerto de Luna when eight men did not come back?

Marone looked at the sun, and it was low,
scarcely above the purple mountains. They seemed
close now. He lengthened his stride again. The
Navajo had told him how his people once had been
pursued by Apaches, and had led the whole Apache
war party into the Sink. There they had been
caught by darkness, and none were ever seen again
according to the Indian's story.

Shad stumbled then, and fell. Dust lifted thickly
about him, clogging his nostrils. Slowly, like a
groggy fighter, he got his knees under him and
using his rifle for a staff, pushed himself to his
feet.

He started on, driven by some blind, brute desire for life. When he fell again he could feel rocks
under his hands. He pulled himself up.

He climbed the steep, winding path toward the
Window in the Rock. Below the far corner of the
Window was the Nest. And in the Nest there was
water. Or so the Navajo had told him.

When he was halfway up the trail he turned and
looked back over the Sink. Far away, he could see
the dust clouds. Four of them. One larger than the
others. Probably there were two men together.

"Still coming," he muttered grimly, "and Lopez
leading them!"

Lopez, damn his soul!

The little devil had guts, though; you had to
give him that. Suddenly, Marone found himself
almost wishing Lopez would win through. The
man was like a wolf. A killer wolf. But he had

guts. And it wasn't just the honest men who had built up this country to what it was today.

Maybe, without the killers and rustlers and badmen, the West would never have been won so soon. Shad Marone remembered some of them: Wild, dangerous men, who went into country where nobody else dared venture. They killed and robbed to live, but they stayed there.

It took iron men for that: Men like Lopez, who was a mongrel of the Santa Fe Trail. Lopez had drunk water from a buffalo track many a time. *Well, so have I,* Shad told himself.

Shad Marone took out his six-shooter and wiped it free of dust. Only then did he start up the trail.

He found the Nest, a hollow among the rocks, sheltered from the wind. The Window loomed above him now, immense, gigantic. Shad stumbled, running, into the Nest. He dropped his rifle and lunged for the water hole, throwing himself on the ground to drink. Then he stared, unbelieving.

Empty!

The earth was dry and parched where the water had been, but only cracked earth remained.

He couldn't believe it. It couldn't be! It couldn't . . . ! Marone came to his feet, glaring wildly about. His eyes were red-rimmed, his face heat-flushed above the black whiskers now filmed with gray dust.

He tried to laugh. Lopez dying down below there, he dying up here! The hard men of the

West, the tough men! He sneered at himself. Both of them now would die, he at the waterhole, Lopez down there in the cloying, clogging dust!

He shook his head. Through the flame-sheathed torment of his brain there came a cool ray of sanity.

There had been water here. The Indian had been right. The cracked earth showed that. But where?

Perhaps a dry season. . . . But no; it had not been a dry season. Certainly no dryer than any other year at this time.

He stared across the place where the pool had been. Rocks, and a few rock cedar, and some heaped up rocks from a small slide. He stumbled across and began clawing at the rocks, pulling, tearing. Suddenly a trickle of water burst through! He got hold of one big rock and in a mad frenzy, tore it from its place. The water shot through then, so suddenly he was knocked to his knees.

He scrambled out of the depression, splashing in the water. Then, lying on his face, he drank, long and greedily.

Finally he rolled away and lay still, panting. Dimly he was conscious of the wind blowing. He crawled to the water again and bathed his face, washing away the dirt and grime. Then, careful as always, he filled his canteen from the fresh water bubbling up from the spring.

If he only had some coffee. . . . But he'd left his food in his saddlebags.

Well, Madge would be all right now. He could go back to her. After this, they wouldn't bother him. He would take her away. They would go to the Blue Mountains in Oregon. He had always liked that country.

The wind was blowing more heavily now, and he could smell the dust. That Navajo hadn't lied. It would be hell down in the Sink. He was above it now, and almost a mile away.

He stared down into the darkness, wondering how far Lopez had been able to get. The others didn't matter; they were weak sisters, who lived on the strength of better men. If they didn't die there they would die elsewhere, and the West could spare them. He got to his feet.

Lopez would hate to die. The ranch he had built so carefully in a piece of the wildest, roughest country was going good. It took a man with guts to settle where he had and make it pay. Shad Marone rubbed the stubble on his jaw. "That last thirty head of his cows I rustled for him brought the best price I ever got!" he remembered thoughtfully. "Too bad there ain't more like him!"

Well, after this night there would be one less. There wouldn't be anything to guide Lopez down there now. A man caught in a thick whirlpool of dust would have no landmarks; there would be nothing to get him out except blind instinct. The Navajos had been clever, leading the Apaches into a trap like that. Odd, that Lopez' mother had been an Apache, too.

Just the same, Marone thought, he had nerve.
He'd shot his way up from the bottom until he had
one of the best ranches.

Shad Marone began to pick up some dead cedar.
He gathered some needles for kindling, and in a
few minutes had a fire going.

Marone took another drink. Somehow, he felt
restless. He got up and walked to the edge of the
Nest. How far had Lopez come? Suppose . . .
Marone gripped his pistol.

Suddenly, he started down the mountain. "The
hell with it!" he muttered.

A stone rattled.

Shad Marone froze, gun in hand.

Lopez, a gray shadow, weaving in the vague
light from the cliff, had a gun in his hand. For a
full minute they stared at each other.

Marone spoke first. "Looks like a dead heat,"
he said.

Lopez said, "How'd you know about that
waterhole?"

"Navajo told me," Shad replied, watching Lopez
like a cat. "You don't look so bad," he added.
"Have a full canteen?"

"No. I'd have been a goner. But my mother
was an Apache. A bunch of them got caught in the
Sink once. That never happened twice to no Apache.
They found this waterhole then, and one down
below. I made the one below, an' then I was
finished. She was a dry hole. But then water began
to run in from a crack in the rock."

"Yeah?" Marone looked at him again. "You got any coffee?"

"Sure."

"Well," Shad holstered his gun, "I've got a fire."

RIDE, YOU TONTO RAIDERS!

CHAPTER ONE

The Seventh Man

The rain, which had been falling steadily for three days, had turned the trail into a sloppy river of mud. Peering through the slanting downpour, Mathurin Sabre cursed himself for the quixotic notion that impelled him to take this special trail to the home of the man that he had gunned down.

Nothing good could come of it, he reflected, yet the thought that the young widow and child might need the money he was carrying had started him upon the long ride from El Paso to the Mogollons. Certainly, neither the bartender nor the hangers-on in the saloon could have been entrusted with that money, and nobody was taking that dangerous ride to the Tonto Basin for fun.

Matt Sabre was no trouble hunter. At various

35

times he had been many things, most of them associated with violence. By birth and inclination he was a Western man, although much of his adult life had been lived far from his native country. He had been a buffalo hunter, a prospector, and for a short time, a two-gun marshal of a tough cattle town. It was his stubborn refusal either to back up or back down that kept him in constant hot water.

Yet some of his trouble derived from something more than that. It stemmed from a dark and bitter drive toward violence—a drive that lay deep within him. He was aware of this drive, and held it in restraint, but at times it welled up and he went smashing into trouble—a big, rugged and dangerous man who fought like a Viking gone berserk, except that he fought coldly and shrewdly.

He was a tall man, heavier than he appeared, and his lean, dark face had a slightly patrician look with high cheekbones and green eyes. His eyes were usually quiet and reserved. He had a natural affinity for horses and weapons. He understood them and they understood him. It had been love of a good horse that brought him to his first act of violence.

He had been buffalo hunting with his uncle, and had interfered with another hunter who was beating his horse. At sixteen a buffalo hunter was a man and expected to stand as one. Matt Sabre stood his ground and shot it out, killing his first man. Had it rested there, all would have been well, but two of the dead man's friends had come

hunting Sabre. Failing to find him, they had beaten
his ailing uncle and stolen the horses. Matt Sabre
trailed them to Mobeetie and killed them both in
the street, taking his horses home.

Then he left the country, to prospect in Mexico,
fight a revolution in Central America, and join the
Foreign Legion in Morocco, from which he deserted after two years. Returning to Texas, he
drove a trail herd up to Dodge, then took a job as
marshal of a town. Six months later in El Paso he
became engaged in an altercation with Billy Curtin,
and Curtin called him a liar and went for his gun.

With that incredible speed that was so much a
part of him, Matt drew his gun and fired. Curtin
hit the floor. An hour later he was summoned to
the dying man's hotel room.

Billy Curtin, his dark, tumbled hair against a
folded blanket, his face drawn and deathly white,
was dying. They told him outside the door that
Curtin might live an hour or even two. He could
not live longer.

Tall, straight and quiet, Sabre walked into the
room and stood by the dying man's bed. Curtin
held a packet wrapped in oilskin. "Five thousand
dollars," he whispered. "Take it to my wife—to
Jenny, on the Pivotrock, in the Mogollons. She's
in—in—trouble."

It was a curious thing, that this dying man
should place a trust in the hands of the man who
had killed him. Sabre stared down at him, frowning a little.

"Why me?" he asked. "You trust me with this? And why should I do it?"

"You—you're a gentleman. I trust—you help her, will you? I—I was a hot—headed fool. Worried—impatient. It wasn't your fault."

The reckless light was gone from the blue eyes, and the light that remained was fading.

"I'll do it, Curtin. You've my word—you've got the word of Matt Sabre."

For an instant then, the blue eyes blazed wide and sharp with knowledge. "You—Sabre?"

Matt nodded, but the light had faded, and Billy Curtin had bunched his herd.

It had been a rough and bitter trip, but there was little further to go. West of El Paso there had been a brush with marauding Apaches. In Silver City two strangely familiar riders had followed him into a saloon and started a brawl. Yet Matt was too wise in the ways of thieves to be caught by so obvious a trick and he had slipped away in the darkness after shooting out the light.

The roan slipped now on the muddy trail, scrambled up and moved on through the trees. Suddenly, in the rain-darkened dusk there was one light, then another.

"Yellowjacket," Matt said, with a sigh of relief. "That means a good bed for us, boy. A good bed and a good feed."

Yellowjacket was a jumping-off place. It was a stage station and a saloon, a livery stable and a

ramshackle hotel. It was a cluster of 'dobe resi-
dences and some false-fronted stores. It bunched
its buildings in a corner of Copper Creek.

It was Galusha Reed's town, and Reed owned
the Yellowjacket Saloon and the Rincon Mine. Sid
Trumbull was town marshal, and he ran the place
for Reed. Wherever Reed rode, Tony Sikes was
close by, and there were some who said that Reed
in turn was owned by Prince McCarran who owned
the big PM brand in the Tonto Basin country.

Matt Sabre stabled his horse and turned to the
slope-shouldered liveryman. "Give him a bait of
corn. Another in the morning."

"Corn?" Simpson shook his head. "We've no
corn."

"You have corn for the freighters' stock, and
corn for the stage horses. Give my horse corn."

Sabre had a sharp ring of authority in his voice
and before he realized it, Simpson was giving the
big roan his corn. He thought about it, and stared
after Sabre. The tall rider was walking away, a
light, long step, easy and free, on the balls of his
feet. And he carried two guns, low hung and tied
down.

Simpson stared, then shrugged. "A bad one,"
he muttered. "Wish he'd kill Sid Trumbull!"

Matt Sabre pushed into the door of the Yellow-
jacket and dropped his saddlebags to the floor.
Then he strode to the bar. "What have you got,
Man? Anything but rye?"

"What's the matter? Ain't rye good enough for you?" Hobbs was sore himself. No man should work so many hours on feet like his.

"Have you brandy? Or some Irish whiskey?"

Hobbs stared. "Mister, where do you think you are? New York?"

"That's all right, Hobbs. I like a man who knows what he likes. Give him some of my cognac."

Matt Sabre turned and glanced at the speaker. He was a tall man, immaculate in black broadcloth, with blond hair slightly wavy, and a rosy complexion. He might have been thirty or older. He wore a pistol on his left side, high up.

"Thanks," Sabre said briefly. "There's nothing better than cognac on a wet night."

"My name is McCarran. I run the PM outfit, east of here. Northeast, to be exact."

Sabre nodded. "My name is Sabre, I run no outfit, but I'm looking for one. Where's the Pivotrock?"

He was a good poker player, men said. His eyes were fast from using guns, and so he saw the sudden glint and the quick caution in Prince McCarran's eyes.

"The Pivotrock? Why, that's a stream over in the Mogollons. There's an outfit over there, all right? A one-horse affair. Why do you ask?"

Sabre cut him off short. "Business with them."

"I see. Well, you'll find it a lonely ride. There's trouble up that way now, some sort of a cattle war."

Matt Sabre tasted his drink. It was good cognac. In fact, it was the best, and he had found none west of New Orleans.

McCarran, his name was. He knew something, too. Curtin had asked him to help his widow. Was the Pivotrock outfit in the war? He decided against asking McCarran, and they talked quietly of the rain and of cattle, then of cognac. "You never acquired a taste for cognac in the West. May I ask where?"

"Paris," Sabre replied, "Marseilles, Fez and Marrakesh."

"You've been around then. Well, that's not uncommon." The blond man pointed toward a heavy-shouldered young man who slept with his head on his arms. "See that chap? Calls himself Camp Gordon. He's a Cambridge man, quotes the classics when he's drunk—which is over half the time—and is one of the best cowhands in the country when he's sober.

"Keys over there, playing the piano, studied in Weimar. He knew Strauss, in Vienna, before he wrote *The Blue Danube*. There's all sorts of men in the West, from belted earls and remittance men to vagabond scum from all corners of the world. They are here a few weeks and they talk the lingo like veterans. Some of the biggest ranches in the West are owned by Englishmen."

Prince McCarran talked to him a few minutes longer, but he learned nothing. Sabre was not evasive, but somehow he gave out no information about himself or his mission. McCarran walked away very thoughtfully. Later, after Matt Sabre was gone, Sid Trumbull came in.

"Sabre?" Trumbull shook his head. "Never heard of him. Keys might know. He knows about ever'body. What's he want on the Pivotrock?"

Lying on his back in bed, Matt Sabre stared up into the darkness and listened to the rain on the window and on the roof. It rattled hard, skeleton fingers against the glass, and he turned restlessly in his bed, frowning as he recalled that quick, guarded expression in the eyes of Prince McCarran.

Who was McCarran, and what did he know? Had Curtin's request that he help his wife been merely the natural request of a dying man, or had he felt that there was a definite need of help? Was something wrong here?

He went to sleep vowing to deliver the money and ride away. Yet even as his eyes closed the last time, he knew he would not do it if there was trouble.

It was still raining, but no longer pouring, when he awakened. He dressed swiftly and checked his guns, his mind taking up his problems where they had been left the previous night.

Camp Gordon, his face puffy from too much drinking and too sound a sleep, staggered down the stairs after him. He grinned woefully at Sabre. "I guess I really hung one on last night," he said. "What I need is to get out of town."

They ate breakfast together, and Gordon's eyes sharpened suddenly at Matt's query of directions to the Pivotrock. "You'll not want to go there, man. Since Curtin ran out they've got their backs to the wall. They are through! Leave it to Galusha Reed for that."

"What's the trouble?"

"Reed claims title to the Pivotrock. Bill Curtin's old man bought it from a Mex who had it from a land grant. Then he made a deal with the Apaches, which seemed to cinch his title. Trouble was, Galusha Reed shows up with a prior claim. He says Fernandez had no grant. That his man Sonoma had a prior one. Old Man Curtin was killed when he fell from his buckboard, and young Billy couldn't stand the gaff. He blew town after Tony Sikes buffaloed him."

"What about his wife?"

Gordon shook his head, then shrugged. Doubt and worry struggled on his face. "She's a fine girl, Jenny Curtin is. The salt of the earth. It's too bad Curtin hadn't a tenth of her nerve. She'll stick, and she swears she'll fight."

"Has she any men?"

"Two. An old man who was with her father-in-law, and a half-breed Apache they call Rado. It used to be Silerado."

Thinking it over, Sabre decided there was much left to be explained. Where had the five thousand dollars come from? Had Billy really run out, or had he gone away to get money to put up a battle? And how did he get it?

"I'm going out," Sabre got to his feet. "I'll have a talk with her."

"Don't take a job there. She hasn't a chance!" Gordon said grimly. "You'd do well to stay away."

"I like fights when one side doesn't have a chance," Matt replied lightly. "Maybe I will ask for a job. A man's got to die sometime, and what better time than fighting when the odds are against him?"

"I like to win," Gordon said flatly. "I like at least a chance."

Matt Sabre leaned over the table, aware that Prince McCarran had moved up behind Gordon, and that a big man with a star was standing near him. "If I decide to go to work for her," Sabre's voice was easy, confident, "then you'd better join us. Our side will win."

"Look here, you!" The man wearing the star, Sid Trumbull, stepped forward. "You either stay in town or get down the trail! There's trouble enough in the Mogollons. Stay out of there."

Matt looked up. "You're telling me?" His voice cracked like a whip. "You're town marshal, Trumbull, not a United States marshal or a sheriff, and if you were a sheriff, it wouldn't matter. It is out of this county. Now suppose you back up and don't step into conversations unless you're invited."

Trumbull's head lowered and his face flushed red. Then he stepped around the table, his eyes narrow and mean. "Listen, you!" His voice was thick with fury. "No two-by-twice cowpoke tells me—!"

"Trumbull," Sabre spoke evenly, "you're asking for it. You aren't acting in line of duty now. You're picking trouble, and the fact that you're marshal won't protect you."

"Protect me?" His fury exploded. "Protect me? Why, you—!"

Trumbull lunged around the table, but Matt sidestepped swiftly and kicked a chair into the marshal's path. Enraged, Sid Trumbull had no chance to avoid it and fell headlong, bloodying his palms on the slivery floor.

Kicking the chair away, he lunged to his feet, and Matt stood facing him, smiling. Camp Gordon was grinning, and Hobbs was leaning his forearms on the bar, watching with relish.

Trumbull stared at his torn palms, then lifted his eyes to Sabre's. Then he started forward, and suddenly, in midstride, his hand swept for his gun.

Sabre palmed his Colt and the gun barked even as it lifted. Stunned, Sid Trumbull stared at his numbed hand. His gun had been knocked spinning, and the .44 slug, hitting the trigger guard, had gone by to rip off the end of Sid's little finger. Dumbly, he stared at the slow drip of blood.

Prince McCarran and Gordon were only two of those who stared, not at the marshal, but at Matt Sabre.

"You throw that gun mighty fast, stranger,"

McCarran said. "Who are you, anyway? There aren't half a dozen men in the country who can throw a gun that fast. I know most of them by sight."

Sabre's eyes glinted coldly. "No? Well, you know another one now. Call it seven men." He spun on his heel and strode from the room. All eyes followed him.

CHAPTER TWO

Coyote Trouble

Matt Sabre's roan headed up Shirt Tail Creek, crossed Bloody Basin and Skeleton Ridge and made the Verde in the vicinity of the hot springs. He bedded down that night in a corner of a cliff near Hardscrabble Creek. It was late when he turned in, and he had lighted no fire.

He had chosen his position well, for behind him the cliff towered, and on his left there was a steep hillside that sloped away toward Hardscrabble Creek. He was almost at the foot of Hardscrabble Mesa, with the rising ground of Deadman Mesa before him. The ground in front sloped away to the creek, and there was plenty of dry wood. The overhang of the cliff protected it from the rain.

Matt Sabre came suddenly awake. For an instant,

47

he lay very still. The sky had cleared, and as he lay on his side he could see the stars. He judged that it was past midnight. Why he had awakened he could not guess, but he saw that the roan was nearer, and the big gelding had his head up and ears pricked.

"Careful, boy!" Sabre warned.

Sliding out of his bed roll he drew on his boots and got to his feet. Feeling out in the darkness, he drew his Winchester near.

He was sitting in absolute blackness due to the cliff's overhang. He knew the boulders and the clumps of cedar were added concealment. The roan would be lost against the blackness of the cliff, but from where he sat he could see some thirty yards of the creek bank and some open ground.

There was subdued movement below and whispering voices. Then silence. Leaving his rifle, Sabre belted on his guns and slid quietly out of the overhang and into the cedars.

After a moment, he heard the sound of movement, and then a low voice: "He can't be far! They said he came this way, and he left the main trail after Fossil Creek."

There were two of them. He waited, standing there among the cedars, his eyes hard and his muscles poised and ready. They were fools. Did they think he was that easy?

He had fought Apaches and Kiowas, and he had fought the Tauregs in the Sahara and the Riffs in the Atlas Mountains. He saw them then, saw their dark figures, moving up the hill, outlined against the pale gravel of the slope.

That hard, bitter thing inside him broke loose, and he could not stand still. He could not wait. They would find the roan, and then they would not leave until they had him. It was now or never. He stepped out, quickly, silently.

"Looking for somebody?"

They wheeled, and he saw the starlight on a pistol barrel, and heard the flat, husky cough of his own gun. One went down, coughing and gasping. The other staggered, then turned and started off in a stumbling run, moaning half in fright, half in pain. He stood there, trying to follow the man, but he lost him in the brush.

He turned back to the fellow on the ground, but did not go near him. He circled wide instead, returning to his horse. He quieted his roan, then lay down. In a few minutes he was dozing.

Daybreak found him standing over the body. The roan was already saddled for the trail. It was one of the two he had seen in Silver City, a lean, dark-faced man with deep lines in his cheeks and a few gray hairs at the temples. There was an old scar, deep and red, over his eye.

Sabre knelt and went through his pockets, taking a few letters and some papers. He stuffed them into his own pockets, then mounted. Riding warily, started up the creek. He rode with his Winchester across his saddle, ready for whatever came. Nothing did.

The morning drew on, the air warm and still after the rain. A fly buzzed around his ears, and he whipped it away with his hat. The roan had a long striding, space-eating walk. It moved out swiftly and surely toward the far purple ranges, dipping down through grassy meadows lined with pines and aspens, with here and there the whispering leaves of a tall cottonwood.

It was a land to dream about, a land perfect for the grazing of either cattle or sheep, a land for a man to live in. Ahead and on his left he could see the towering Mogollon Rim, and it was beyond this Rim, up on the plateau, that he would find the Pivotrock. He skirted a grove of rustling aspen and looked down a long valley.

For the first time he saw cattle—fat, contented cattle, fat from the rich grass of these bottomlands. Once, far off, he glimpsed a rider, but he made no effort to draw near, wanting only to find the trail to the Pivotrock.

A wide-mouthed canyon opened from the northeast and he turned the roan and started up the creek that ran down it. Now he was climbing, and from the look of the country he would climb nearly three thousand feet to reach the Rim. Yet he had been told there was a trail ahead and he pushed on.

The final eight hundred feet to the Rim was by a

switchback trail that had him climbing steadily, yet the air on the plateau atop the Rim was amazingly fresh and clear. He pushed on, seeing a few scattered cattle, and then he saw a crude wooden sign by the narrow trail. It read:

PIVOTROCK . . . 1 MILE

The house was low and sprawling, lying on a flat-topped knoll with the long barns and sheds built on three sides of a square. The open side faced the Rim and the trail up which he was riding. There were cottonwoods, pine, and fir backing up the buildings. He could see the late afternoon sunlight glistening on the coats of the saddlestock in the corral.

An old man stepped from the stable with a carbine in his hands. "All right, stranger. You stop where you are. What you want here?"

Matt Sabre grinned. Lifting his hand carefully, he pushed back his flat-brimmed hat. "Huntin' Mrs. Jenny Curtin," he said. "I've got news." He hesitated. "Of her husband."

The carbine muzzle lowered. "Of *him?* What news would there be of him?"

"Not good news," Sabre told him. "He's dead."

Surprisingly, the old man seemed relieved. "Right," he said briefly. "I reckon we figured he was dead. How'd it happen?"

Sabre hesitated. "He picked a fight in a saloon in El Paso, then drew too slow."

"He was never fast." The old man studied him. "My name's Tom Judson. Now, you sure didn't come all the way here from El Paso to tell us Billy was dead. What did you come for?"

"I'll tell Mrs. Curtin that. However, they tell me down the road you've been with her a long time, so you might as well know. I brought her some money. Bill Curtin gave it to me on his death bed, asked me to bring it to her. It's five thousand dollars."

"Five thousand?" Judson stared. "Reckon Bill must have set some store by you to trust you with it. Know him long?"

Sabre shook his head. "Only a few minutes. A dying man hasn't much choice."

A door slammed up at the house, and they both turned. A slender girl was walking toward them, and the sunlight caught the red in her hair. She wore a simple cotton dress, but her figure was trim and neat. Ahead of her dashed a boy who might have been five or six. He lunged at Sabre, then slid to a stop and stared up at him, then at his guns.

"Howdy, Old Timer!" Sabre said, smiling. "Where's your spurs?"

The boy was startled and shy. He drew back, surprised at the question. "I—I've got no spurs!"

"What? A cowhand without spurs? We'll have to fix that." He looked up. "How are you, Mrs. Curtin? I'm Mathurin Sabre, Matt for short. I'm afraid I've some bad news for you."

Her face paled a little, but her chin lifted. "Will

you come to the house, Mr. Sabre? Tom, put his horse in the corral, will you?''

The living room of the ranch house was spacious and cool. There were Navajo rugs upon the floor, and the chairs and the divan were beautifully tanned cowhide. He glanced around appreciatively, enjoying the coolness after his hot ride in the Arizona sun, liking the naturalness of this girl, standing in the home she had created.

She faced him abruptly. ''Perhaps you'd better tell me now, there's no use pretending or putting a bold face on it when I have to be told.''

As quickly and quietly as possible, he explained. When he was finished her face was white and still. ''I—I was afraid of this. When he rode away I knew he would never come back. You see, he thought—he believed he had failed me, failed his father.''

Matt drew the oilskin packet from his pocket. ''He sent you this. He said it was five thousand dollars. He said to give it to you.''

She took it, staring at the package, and tears welled into her eyes. ''Yes.'' Her voice was so low that Matt scarcely heard it. ''He would do this. He probably felt it was all he could do for me, for us. You see,'' Jenny Curtin's eyes lifted, ''we're in a fight, and a bad one. This is war money.

''I—guess Billy thought—well, he was no fighter himself, and this might help, might compensate. You're probably wondering about all this.''

"No," he said. "I'm not. And maybe I'd better go out with the boys now. You'll want to be alone."

"Wait!" Her fingers caught his sleeve. "I want you to know, since you were with him when he died, and you have come all this way to help us. There was no trouble with Billy and me. It was— well, he thought he was a coward. He thought he had failed me.

"We've had trouble with Galusha Reed in Yellowjacket. Tony Sikes picked a fight with Billy. He wanted to kill him, and Billy wouldn't fight. He—he backed down. Everybody said he was a coward, and he ran. He went—away."

Matt Sabre frowned thoughtfully, staring at the floor. The boy who picked a fight with him, who dared him, who went for his gun, was no coward. Trying to prove something to himself? Maybe. But no coward.

"Ma'am," he said abruptly, "you're his widow. The mother of his child. There's something you should know. Whatever else he was, I don't know. I never knew him long enough. But that man was no coward. Not even a little bit!

"You see," Matt hesitated, feeling the falseness of his position, not wanting to tell this girl that he had killed her husband, yet not wanting her to think him a coward; "I saw his eyes when he went for his gun. I was there, Ma'am, and saw it all. Bill Curtin was no coward."

*　　*　　*

Hours later, lying in his bunk, he thought of it, and the five thousand was still a mystery. Where had it come from? How had Curtin come by it?

He turned over and after a few minutes, went to sleep. Tomorrow he would be riding.

The sunlight was bright the next morning when he finally rolled out of bed. He bathed and shaved, taking his time, enjoying the sun on his back, and feeling glad he was footloose again. He was in the bunkhouse belting on his guns when he heard the horses. He stepped to the door and glanced out.

Neither the dark-faced Rado nor Judson were about, and there were three riders in the yard. One of them he recognized as a man from Yellowjacket, and the tallest of the riders was Galusha Reed. He was a big man, broad and thick in the body without being fat. His jaw was brutal.

Jenny Curtin came out on the steps. "Ma'am," Reed said abruptly, "we're movin' you off this land. We're goin' to give you ten minutes to pack, an' one of my boys'll hitch the buckboard for you. This here trouble's gone on long enough, an' mine's the prior claim to this land. You're gettin' off!"

Jenny's eyes turned quickly toward the stable, but Reed shook his head. "You needn't look for Judson or the breed. We watched until we seen them away from here, an' some of my boys are coverin' the trail. We're tryin' to get you off here without any trouble."

"You can turn around and leave, Mr. Reed. I'm not going!"

"I reckon you are," Reed said patiently. "We know that your man's dead. We just can't put up with you squattin' on our range."

"This happens to be my range, and I'm staying."

Reed chuckled. "Don't make us put you off, Ma'am. Don't make us get rough. Up here," he waved a casual hand, "we can do anything we want, and nobody the wiser. You're leavin', as of now."

Matt Sabre stepped out of the bunkhouse and took three quick steps toward the riders. He was cool and sure of himself, but he could feel the jumping invitation to trouble surging up inside him. He fought it down, and held himself still for an instant. Then he spoke.

"Reed, you're a fat-headed fool and a bully. You ride up here to take advantage of a woman because you think she's helpless. Well, she's not. Now you three turn your horses—turn 'em mighty careful—and start down the trail. And don't you ever set foot on this place again!"

Reed's face went white, then dark with anger. He leaned forward a little. "So you're still here? Well, we'll give you a chance to run. Get goin'!"

Matt Sabre walked forward another step. He could feel the eagerness pushing up inside him, and his eyes held the three men, and he saw the eyes of one widen with apprehension.

"Watch it, Boss! Watch it!"

"That's right, Reed. Watch it. You figured to find this girl alone. Well, she's not alone. Furthermore, if she'll take me on as a hand, I'll stay. I'll stay until you're out of the country or dead. You can have it either way you want.

"There's three of you. I like that. That evens us up. If you want to feed buzzards, just edge that hand another half inch toward your gun and you can. That goes for the three of you."

He stepped forward again. He was jumping with it now—that old drive for combat welling up within him. Inside he was trembling, but his muscles were steady and his mind was cool and ready. His fingers spread and he moved forward again.

"Come on, you mangy coyotes! Let's see if you've got the nerve. *Reach!*"

Reed's face was still and cold. His mouth looked pinched, and his eyes were wide. Some sixth sense warned him that this was different. This was death he was looking at, and Galusha Reed suddenly realized he was no gambler when the stakes were so high.

He could see the dark eagerness that was driving this cool man; he could see beyond the coolness on his surface the fierceness of his readiness; inside he went sick and cold at the thought.

"Boss!" the man at his side whispered hoarsely, "let's get out of here. This man's poison!"

Galusha Reed slowly eased his hand forward to the pommel of the saddle. "So, Jenny, you're hiring gunfighters? Is that the way you want it?"

"I think you hired them first," she replied coolly. "Now you'd better go."

"On the way back," Sabre suggested, "you might stop in Hardscrabble Canyon and pick up the body of one of your killers. He guessed wrong last night."

Reed stared at him. "I don't know what you mean," he flared. "I sent out no killer."

Matt Sabre watched the three men ride down the trail and he frowned. There had been honest doubt in Reed's eyes, but if he had not sent the two men after him, who had? Those men had been in Silver City and El Paso, yet they also knew this country, and knew someone in Yellowjacket. Maybe they had not come after him, but had first followed Bill Curtin.

He turned and smiled at the girl. "Coyotes," he said, shrugging. "Not much heart in them."

She was staring at him strangely. "You—you'd have killed them, wouldn't you? Why?"

He shrugged. "I don't know. Maybe it's because—well, I don't like to see men take advantage of a woman alone. Anyway," he smiled, "Reed doesn't impress me as a good citizen."

"He's a dangerous enemy." She came down from the steps. "Did you mean what you said, Mr. Sabre? I mean about staying here and working for me? I need men, although I must tell you that you've small chance of winning, and it's rather a lonely fight."

"Yes, I meant it." Did he mean it? Of course. He remembered the old Chinese proverb: if you save a person's life he becomes your responsibility.

That wasn't the case here, but he had killed this girl's husband, and the least he could do would be to stay until she was out of trouble.

Was that all he was thinking of? "I'll stay," he said. "I'll see you through this. I've been fighting all my life and it would be a shame to stop now. And I've fought for lots less reasons."

CHAPTER THREE

Hot Night in Yellowjacket

Throughout the morning he worked around the place. He worked partly because there was much to be done and partly because he wanted to think.

The horses in the remuda were held on the home place, and were in good shape. Also, they were better than the usual ranch horses, for some of them showed a strong Morgan strain. He repaired the latch on the stable door, and walked around the place, sizing it up from every angle, studying all the approaches.

With his glasses he studied the hills and searched the notches and canyons wherever he could see them. Mentally, he formed a map of all that terrain within reach of his glass.

It was mid-afternoon before Judson and Rado

61

returned, and they had talked with Jenny before he saw them.

"Howdy," Judson was friendly, but his eyes studied Sabre with care. "Miss Jenny tells me you run Reed off. That you're aimin' to stay on here."

"That's right. I'll stay until she's out of trouble, if she'll have me. I don't like being pushed around."

"No, neither do I." Judson was silent for several minutes, and then he turned his eyes on Sabre. "Don't you be gettin' any ideas about Miss Jenny. She's a fine girl."

Matt looked up angrily. "And don't you be getting any ideas," he said coldly. "I'm helping her, the same as you are, and we'll work together. As to personal things, leave them alone. I'll only say that when this fight is over, I'm hitting the trail."

"All right," Judson said mildly. "We can use help."

Three days passed smoothly. Matt threw himself into the work of the ranch, and he worked feverishly. Even he could not have said why he worked so desperately hard. He dug postholes and fenced an area in the long meadow near the seeping springs in the bottom.

Then, working with Rado, he rounded up the cattle nearest the Rim and pushed them back behind the fence. The grass was thick and deep there and would stand a lot of grazing, for the meadow wound back up the canyon for some distance. He carried a running iron and branded stock wherever he found it required.

As the ranch had been short-handed for a year, there was much to do. Evenings, he mended gear and worked around the place, and at night he slept soundly. During all this time he saw nothing of Jenny Curtin.

He saw nothing of her, but she was constantly in his thoughts. He remembered her as he had seen her that first night, standing in the living room of the house, listening to him, her eyes, wide and dark, upon his face. He remembered her facing Galusha Reed and his riders from the steps.

Was he staying on because he believed he owed her a debt, or because of her?

Here and there around the ranch, Sabre found small, intangible hints of the sort of man Curtin must have been. Judson had liked him, and so had the halfbreed. He had been gentle with horses. He had been thoughtful. Yet he had hated and avoided violence. Slowly, rightly or wrongly Matt could not tell, a picture was forming in his mind of a fine young man who had been totally out of place.

Western birth, but born for peaceful and quiet ways, he had been thrown into a cattle war and had been aware of his own inadequacy. Matt was thinking of that, and working at a rawhide riata, when Jenny came up.

He had not seen her approach or he might have avoided her, but she was there beside him before he realized it.

"You're working hard, Mr. Sabre."

"To earn my keep, Ma'am. There's a lot to do, I find, and I like to keep busy." He turned the riata and studied it.

"You know, there's something I've been wanting to talk to you about. Maybe it's none of my affair, but young Billy is going to grow up, and he's going to ask questions about his Dad. You aren't going to be able to fool him. Maybe you know what this is all about and maybe I'm mounting on the off-side, but it seems to me that Bill Curtin went to El Paso to get that money for you.

"I think he realized he was no fighting man, and that the best thing he could do was to get that money so he could hire gunfighters. It took nerve to do what he did, and I think he deliberately took what Sikes handed him because he knew that if Sikes killed him you'd never get that money.

"Maybe along the way to El Paso he began to wonder, and maybe he picked that fight down there with the idea of proving to himself that he did have the nerve to face a gun."

She did not reply, but stood there, watching his fingers work swiftly and evenly, plaiting the leather.

"Yes," she said finally, "I thought of that. Only I can't imagine where he got the money. I hesitate to use it without knowing."

"Don't be foolish," he said irritably. "Use it. Nobody would put it to better use, and you need gun-hands."

"But who would work for me?" Her voice was low and bitter. "Galusha Reed has seen to it that no one will."

"Maybe if I rode in I could find some men." He was thinking of Camp Gordon, the Shakespeare-quoting English cowhand. "I believe I know one man."

"There's a lot to be done. Jud tells me you've been doing the work of three men."

Matt Sabre got to his feet. She stepped back a little, suddenly aware of how tall he was. She was tall for a girl, yet she came no farther than his lips. She drew back a little at the thought. Her eyes dropped to his guns. He always wore them, always low and tied down.

"Judson said you were a fast man with a gun. He said you had the mark of the—of the gunfighter."

"Probably." He found no bitterness at the thought. "I've used guns. Guns and horses, they are about all I've known."

"Where were you in the Army? I've watched you walk and ride and you show military training."

"Oh, several places. Africa mostly."

"Africa?" She was amazed. "You've been there?"

He nodded. "Desert and mountain country. Morocco and the Sahara, all the way to Timbuktu and Lake Chad, fighting most of the time." It was growing dark in the shed where they were standing. He moved out into the dusk. A few stars had already appeared, and the red glow that was in the west beyond the Rim was fading.

"Tomorrow I'll ride in and have a look around. You'd better keep the other men close by."

Dawn found him well along on the trail to Yellowjacket. It was a long ride, and he skirted the trail most of the time, having no trust in well-traveled ways at such a time. The air was warm and bright, and he noticed a few head of Pivotrock steers that had been overlooked in the rounding up of cattle along the Rim.

He rode ready for trouble, his Winchester across his saddle bows, his senses alert. Keeping the roan well back under the trees, he had the benefit of the evergreen needles that formed a thick carpet and muffled the sound of his horse's hoofs.

Yet as he rode, he considered the problem of the land grant. If Jenny were to retain her land and be free of trouble he must look into the background of the grant, and see which had the prior and best claim, Fernandez or Sonoma.

Next, he must find out, if possible, where Bill Curtin had obtained that five thousand dollars. Some might think that the fact he had it was enough, and that now his wife had it, but it was not enough if Bill had sold any rights to water or land on the ranch, or if he had obtained the money in some way that would reflect upon Jenny or her son.

When those things were done he could ride on

about his business, for by that time he would have worked out the problem of Galusha Reed.

In the few days he had been on the Pivotrock he had come to love the place, and while he had avoided Jenny, he had not avoided young Billy. The youngster had adopted him, and had stayed with him hour after hour.

To keep him occupied, Matt had begun teaching him how to plait rawhide, and so as he mended riatas and repaired bridles, the youngster had sat beside him, working his fingers clumsily through the intricacies of the plaiting.

It was with unease that he recalled his few minutes alone with Jenny. He shifted his seat in the saddle and scowled. It would not do for him to think of her as anything but Curtin's widow. The widow, he reflected bitterly, of the man he had killed.

What would he say when he learned of *that?* He avoided the thought, yet it remained in the back of his mind, and he shook his head, wanting to forget it. Sooner or later she would know. If he did not finally tell her himself, then he was sure that Reed would let her know.

Avoiding the route by way of Hardscrabble, Matt Sabre turned due south, crossing the eastern end of the mesa and following an old trail across Whiterock and Polles Mesa, crossing the East Verde at Rock Creek. Then he cut through Boardinghouse Canyon to Bullspring, crossing the main stream of the Verde near Tangle Peak. It was a longer way around by a few miles, but Sabre rode with care, watching the country as he travelled. It was very late when he walked his roan into the parched street of Yellowjacket.

He had a hunch and he meant to follow it through. During his nights in the bunkhouse he had talked much with Judson, and from him heard of Pepito Fernandez, a grandson of the man who sold the land to Old Man Curtin.

Swinging down from his horse at the livery stable, he led him inside. Simpson walked over to meet him, his eyes searching Sabre's face. "Man, you've a nerve with you. Reed's wild. He came back to town blazing mad, and Trumbull's telling everybody what you can expect."

Matt smiled at the man. "I expected that. Where do you stand?"

"Well," Simpson said grimly, "I've no liking for Trumbull. He carries himself mighty big around town, and he's not been friendly to me and mine. I reckon, Mister, I've rare been so pleased as when you made a fool of him in yonder. It was better than the killing of him, although he's that coming, sure enough."

"Then take care of my horse, will you? And a slip knot to tie him with."

"Sure, and he'll get corn, too. I reckon any horse you ride would need corn."

Matt Sabre walked out on the street. He was wearing dark jeans and a gray wool shirt. His

black hat was pulled low, and he merged well with
the shadows. He'd see Pepito first, and then look
around a bit. He wanted Camp Gordon.

Thinking of that, he turned back into the stable.
"Saddle Gordon's horse, too. He'll be going back
with me."

"Him?" Simpson stared. "Man, he's dead drunk
and has been for days!"

"Saddle his horse. He'll be with me when I'm
back, and if you know another one or two, good
hands who would use a gun if need be, let them
know I'm hiring and there's money to pay them.
Fighting wages if they want." . . .

In the back office of the Yellowjacket, three
men sat over Galusha Reed's desk. There was
Reed himself, Sid Trumbull and Prince McCarran.

"Do you think Tony can take him?" Reed asked.
"You've seen the man draw, Prince."

"He'll take him. But it will be close—too close.
I think what we'd better do is have Sid posted
somewhere close by."

"Leave me out of it." Sid looked up from
under his thick eyebrows. "I want no more of the
man. Let Tony have him."

"You won't be in sight," McCarran said dryly,
"or in danger. You'll be upstairs over the hotel,
with a Winchester."

Trumbull looked up and touched his thick lips
with his tongue. Killing was not new to him, yet
the way this man accepted it always appalled him
a little.

"All right," he agreed, "like I say, I've no love for him."

"We'll have him so you'll get a flanking shot. Make it count and make it the first time. But wait until the shooting starts."

The door opened softly and Sikes stepped in. He was a lithe, dark-skinned man who moved like an animal. He had graceful hands, restless hands. He wore a white buckskin vest worked with red quills and beads. "Boss, he's in town. Sabre's here."

He had heard them.

Reed let his chair legs down, leaning forward. "*Here?* In town?"

"That's right. I just saw him outside the Yellowjacket." Sikes started to build a cigarette. "He's got nerve. Plenty of it."

The door sounded with a light tap, and at a word, Keys entered. He was a slight man with gray hair and a quiet, scholar's face.

"I remember him now, Prince," he said. "Matt Sabre. I'd been trying to place the name. He was marshal of Mobeetie for awhile. He's killed eight or nine men."

"That's right!" Trumbull looked up sharply. "Mobeetie! Why didn't I remember that? They say Wes Hardin rode out of town once when Sabre sent him word he wasn't wanted."

Sikes turned his eyes on McCarran. "You want him now?"

McCarran hesitated, studying the polished toe of his boot. Sabre's handling of Trumbull had made friends in town, and also his championing of the cause of Jenny Curtin. Whatever happened must be seemingly above board and in the clear, and he wanted to be where he could be seen at the time, and Reed also.

"No, not now. We'll wait." He smiled. "One thing about a man of his courage and background, if you send for him, he'll always come to you."

"But how will he come?" Keys asked softly. "That's the question."

McCarran looked around irritably. He had forgotten Keys was in the room and had said far more than he had intended. "Thanks, Keys. That will be all. And remember—nothing will be said about anything you've heard here."

"Certainly not," Keys smiled and walked to the door and out of the room.

Reed stared after him. "I don't like that fellow, Prince. I wouldn't trust him."

"Him? He's interested in nothing but that piano and enough liquor to keep himself mildly embalmed. Don't worry about him."

CHAPTER FOUR

Fugitive

Matt Sabre turned away from the Yellowjacket after a brief survey of the saloon. Obviously, something was doing elsewhere for none of the men were present in the big room. He hesitated, considering the significance of that, and then turned down a dark alleyway and walked briskly along until he came to an old rail fence.

Following this past rustling cottonwoods and down a rutted road, he turned past a barn and cut across another road toward a 'dobe where the windows glowed with a faint light.

The door opened to his knock and a dark, Indian-like face showed briefly. In rapid Spanish, he asked for Pepito. After a moment's hesitation, the door widened and he was invited inside.

The room was large, and at one side a small fire burned in the blackened fireplace. An oilcloth-covered table with a coal oil light stood in the middle of the room, and on a bed at one side a man snored peacefully.

A couple of dark-eyed children ceased their playing to look up at him. The woman called out and a blanket pushed aside and a slender, dark-faced youth entered the room, pulling his belt tight.

"Pepito Fernandez? I am Matt Sabre."

"I have heard of you, señor."

Briefly, he explained why he had come, and Pepito listened, then shook his head. "I do not know, señor. The grant was long ago, and we are no longer rich. My father," he shrugged, "he liked the spending of money when he was young."

He hesitated, considering that. Then he said carelessly, "I too, like the spending of money. What else is it for? But no, señor, I do not think there are papers. My father, he told me much of the grant, and I am sure the Sonomas had no strong claim."

"If you remember anything, will you let us know?" Sabre asked. Then a thought occured to him. "You're a vaquero? Do you want a job?"

"A job?" Pepito studied him thoughtfully. "At the Señora Curtin's ranch?"

"Yes. As you know, there may be much trouble. I am working there, and tonight I shall take one other man back with me. If you would like the job, it is yours.''

Pepito shrugged. "Why not? Señor Curtin, the old one, he gave me my first horse. He gave me a rifle, too. He was a good one, and the son also.''

"Better meet me outside of town where the trail goes between the Buttes. You know the place?''

"Si, señor. I will be there.''

Keys was idly playing the piano when Matt Sabre opened the door and stepped into the room. His quick eyes placed Keys, Hobbs at the bar, Camp Gordon fast asleep with his head on a table, and a half dozen other men. Yet as he walked to the bar, a rear door opened and Tony Sikes stepped into the room.

Sabre had never before seen the man, yet he knew him from Judson's apt and careful description. Sikes was not as tall as Sabre, yet more slender. He had the wiry, stringy build that is made for speed, and quick, smooth-flowing fingers. His muscles were relaxed and easy, but knowing such men, Matt recognized danger when he saw it. Sikes had seen him at once, and he moved to the bar nearby.

All eyes were on the two of them, for the story of Matt's whipping of Trumbull and his defiance of Reed had swept the country. Yet Sikes merely smiled and Matt glanced at him. "Have a drink?''

Tony Sikes nodded. "I don't mind if I do.'' Then he added, his voice low, and his dark, yellowish eyes on Matt's with a faintly sardonic, faintly amused look, "I never mind drinking with a man I'm going to kill."

Sabre shrugged. "Neither do I." He found himself liking Sikes' direct approach. "Although perhaps I have the advantage. I choose my own time to drink and to kill. You wait for orders."

Tony Sikes felt in his vest pocket for cigarette papers and began to roll a smoke. "You will wait for me, compadre. I know you're the type."

They drank, and as they drank, the door opened and Galusha Reed stepped out. His face darkened angrily when he saw the two standing at the bar together, but he was passing without speaking when a thought struck him. He stopped and turned.

"I wonder," he said loudly enough for all in the room to hear, "what Jenny Curtin will say when she finds out her new hand is the man who killed her husband?"

Every head came up, and Sabre's face whitened. Where the faces had been friendly or noncomittal, now they were sharp-eyed and attentive. Moreover, he knew that Jenny was well liked, as Curtin had been. Now, they would be his enemies.

"I wonder just why you came here, Sabre? After killing the girl's husband, why would you come to her ranch? Was it to profit from your murder? To steal what little she has left? Or is it for the girl herself?"

Matt struggled to keep his temper. After a minute he said casually, "Reed, it was you ordered her off her ranch today. I'm here for one reason, and one alone. To see that she keeps her ranch and that no yellow bellied thievin' lot of coyotes ride over and take it away from her!"

Reed stood flat-footed, facing Sabre. He was furious, and Matt could feel the force of his rage. It was almost a physical thing pushing against him. Close beside him was Sikes. If Reed chose to go for a gun, Sikes could grab Matt's left arm and jerk him off-balance. Yet Matt was ready even for that, and again that black force was rising within him, that driving urge toward violence.

He spoke again and his voice was soft and almost purring. "Make up your mind, Reed. If you want to die, you can right here. You make another remark to me and I'll drive every word of it back down that fat throat of yours! Reach and I'll kill you. If Sikes wants in on this, he's welcome!"

Tony Sikes spoke softly, too. "I'm out of it, Sabre. I only fight my own battles. When I come after you, I'll be alone."

Galusha Reed hesitated. For an instant, counting on Sikes, he had been tempted. Now he hesitated, then turned abruptly and left the room.

Ignoring Sikes, Sabre downed his drink and crossed to Camp Gordon. He shook him. "Come on, Camp, I'm puttin' you to bed."

Gordon did not move. Sabre stooped and slipped an arm around the big Englishman's shoulders and hoisting him to his feet, started for the door. At the door, he turned. "I'll be seeing you, Sikes!"

Tony lifted his glass, his hat pushed back, "Sure," he said. "And I'll be alone."

It was not until after he had said it that he remembered Sid Trumbull and the plans made in the back room. His face darkened a little and his liquor suddenly tasted bad. He put his glass down carefully on the bar and turned, walking through the back door.

Prince McCarran was alone, idly riffling the cards and smoking. "I won't do it, Prince," Sikes said. "You've got to leave that killing to me and me alone."

Matt Sabre, with Camp Gordon lashed to the saddle of a led horse, met Pepito in the darkness of the space between the Buttes. Pepito spoke softly, and Sabre called back to him. As the Mexican rode out he glanced once at Gordon, and then the three rode on together. It was late the following morning when they reached the Pivotrock. All was quiet—too quiet.

Camp Gordon was sober and swearing, "Shanghaied!" His voice exploded with violence. "You've a nerve, Sabre. Turn me loose so I can start back. I'm having no part of this."

Gordon was tied to his horse so he would not fall off, but Matt only grinned. "Sure, I'll turn you loose. But you said you ought to get out of town awhile, and this was the best way. I've brought you here," he said gravely, but his eyes were twinkling, "for your own good. It's time you had some fresh, mountain air, some cold milk, some—"

"Milk?" Gordon exploded. "Milk, you say? I'll not touch the stuff! Turn me loose and give me a gun and I'll have your hide!"

"And leave this ranch for Reed to take? Reed and McCarran?"

Gordon stared at him from bloodshot eyes, eyes that were suddenly attentive. "Did you say McCarran? What's he got to do with this?"

"I wish I knew. But I've a hunch he's in up to his ears. I think he has strings on Reed."

Gordon considered that. "He may have." He watched Sabre undoing the knots. "It's a point I hadn't considered. But why?"

"You've known him longer than I have. Somebody had two men follow Curtin out of the country to kill him, and I don't believe Reed did it. Does that make sense?"

"No." Gordon swung stiffly to the ground. He swayed a bit, clinging to the stirrup leather. He glanced sheepishly at Matt. "I guess I'm a mess." A surprised look crossed his face. "Say, I'm hungry! I haven't been hungry in weeks."

With four hands besides himself, work went on swiftly. Yet Matt Sabre's mind would not rest. The five thousand dollars was a problem, and also there was the Grant. Night after night he led Pepito to talk of the memories of his father and grandfather, and little by little, he began to know the men. An idea was shaping in his mind, but as yet there was little on which to build.

In all this time there was no sign of Reed. On two occasions riders had been seen, apparently scouting. Cattle had been swept from the Rim edge and pushed back, accounting for all or nearly all the strays he had seen on his ride to Yellowjacket.

Matt was restless, sure that when trouble came it would come with a rush. It was like Reed to do things that way. By now he was certainly aware that Camp Gordon and Pepito Fernandez had been added to the roster of hands at Pivotrock.

"Spotted a few head over near Baker Butte," Camp said one morning. "How'd it be if I drifted that way and looked them over?"

"We'll go together," Matt replied. "I've been wanting to look around there, and there's been no chance."

The morning was bright and they rode swiftly, putting miles behind them, alert to all the sights and sounds of the high country above the Rim. Careful as they were, they were no more than a hundred yards from the riders when they saw them. There were five men, and in the lead rode Sid Trumbull and a white-mustached stranger.

There was no possibility of escaping unnoticed. They pushed on toward the advancing riders who drew up and waited. Sid Trumbull's face was sharp with triumph when he saw Sabre.

"Here's your man, Marshal!" he said, with satisfaction. "The one with the black hat is Sabre."

"What's this all about?" Matt asked quietly. He had already noticed the badge the man wore. But he noticed something else. The man looked to be a competent, upstanding officer.

"You're wanted in El Paso. I'm Rafe Collins, Deputy United States Marshal. We're making an inquiry into the killing of Bill Curtin."

Camp's lips tightened and he looked sharply at Sabre. When Reed had brought out this fact in the saloon, Gordon had been dead drunk.

"That was a fair shooting, Marshal. Curtin picked the fight and drew on me."

"You expect us to believe that?" Trumbull was contemptuous. "Why, he hadn't the courage of a mouse! He backed down from Sikes only a few days before. He wouldn't draw on any man with two hands!"

"He drew on me." Matt Sabre realized he was fighting two battles here—one to keep from being arrested, the other to keep Gordon's respect and assistance. "My idea is that he only backed out of a fight with Sikes because he had a job to do, and knew Sikes would kill him."

"That's a likely yarn!" Trumbull nodded to him. "There's your man. It's your job, Marshal."

Collins was obviously irritated. That he entertained no great liking for Trumbull was obvious. Yet he had his duty to do. Before he could speak, Sabre spoke again.

"Marshal, I've reason to believe that some influence has been brought to bear to discredit me and to get me out of the country for awhile. Can't I give you my word that I'll report to El Paso when things are straightened out? My word is good, and that there are many in El Paso who know that."

"Sorry." Collins was regretful. "I've my duty and my orders."

"I understand that," Sabre replied. "I also have my duty. It is to see that Jenny Curtin is protected from those who are trying to force her off her range. I intend to do exactly that."

"Your duty?" Collins eyed him coldly but curiously. "After killing her husband?"

"That's reason enough, sir!" Sabre replied flatly. "The fight was not my choice. Curtin pushed it, and he was excited, worried, and overwrought. Yet he asked me on his death bed to deliver a package to his wife and to see that she was protected. That duty, sir," his eyes met those of Collins, "comes first."

"I'd like to respect that," Collins admitted. "You seem like a gentleman, sir, and it's a quality that's too rare. Unfortunately, I have my orders. However, it should not take long to straighten this out if it was a fair shooting."

"All these rats need," Sabre replied, "is a few days!" He knew there was no use arguing. His horse was fast, and dense pines bordered the road. He needed a minute, and that badly.

As if divining his thought, Camp Gordon suddenly pushed his gray between Matt and the marshal, and almost at once, Matt lashed out with his toe and booted Trumbull's horse in the ribs. The bronc went to bucking furiously. Whipping his horse around, Matt slapped the spurs to his ribs and in two startled jumps he was off and deep into the pines running like a startled deer.

Behind him a shot rang out, and then another. Both cut the brush over his head, but the horse was running now, and he was mounted well. He had started into the trees at right angles, but swung his horse immediately and headed back toward the Pivotrock. Corduroy Wash opened off to his left and he turned the black and pushed rapidly into the mouth of the wash.

Following it for almost a mile, he came out and paused briefly in the clump of trees that crowned a small ridge. He stared back.

A string of riders stretched out on his back trail, but they were scattered out, hunting for tracks. A lone horseman sat not far from them, obviously watching. Matt grinned, that would be Gordon, and he was all right.

Turning his horse, Matt followed a shelf of rock until it ran out, rode off it into thick sand, and then into the pines with their soft bed of needles that left almost no tracks.

Cinch Hook Butte was off to his left, and nearer, on his right, Twenty-Nine Mile Butte. Keeping his horse headed between them, but bearing steadily northwest, he headed for the broken country around

Horsetank Wash. Descending into the canyon he rode northwest, then circled back south and entered the even deeper Calfpen Canyon.

Here, in a nest of boulders, he staked out his horse on a patch of grass. Rifle across his knees, he rested. After an hour, he worked his way to the ledge at the top of the canyon, but nowhere could he see any sign of pursuit. Nor could he hear the sound of hoofs.

There was water in the bottom of Calfpen, not far from where he had left his horse. Food was something else again. He shucked a handful of chia seeds and ate a handful of them, along with the nuts of a piñon.

Obviously, the attempted arrest had been brought about by either the influence of Galusha Reed or Prince McCarran. In either case he was now a fugitive. If they went on to the ranch, Rafe Collins would have a chance to talk to Jenny Curtin. Matt felt sick when he thought of the marshal telling her that it was he who had killed her husband. That she must find out sooner or later, he knew, but he wanted to tell her himself, in his own good time.

CHAPTER FIVE

Bushwhack Bait

When dusk had fallen he mounted the black and worked his way down Calfpen toward Fossil Springs. As he rode, he was considering his best course. Whether taken by Collins or not, he was not now at the ranch and they might choose this time to strike. With some reason they might believe he had left the country. Indeed, there was every chance that Reed actually believed he had come here with some plan of his own to get the Curtin ranch.

Finally, he bedded down for the night in a draw above Fossil Springs and slept soundly until daylight brought a sun that crept over the rocks and shone upon his eyes. He was up, made a light breakfast of coffee and jerked beef, and then saddled up.

Wherever he went now he could expect hostility. Doubt or downright suspicion would have developed as a result of Reed's accusation in Yellowjacket, and the country would know the United States Marshal was looking for him.

Debating his best course, Matt Sabre headed west through the mountains. By nightfall the following day, he was camped in the ominous shadow of Turret Butte where only a few years before Major Randall had ascended the peak in darkness to surprise a camp of Apaches.

Awakening at the break of dawn Matt scouted the vicinity of Yellowjacket with care.

There was some movement in town—more than usual at that hour. He observed a long line of saddled horses at the hitch rails. He puzzled over this, studying it narrow-eyed from the crest of a ridge through his glasses. Marshal Collins could not yet have returned, hence this must be some other movement. That it was organized was obvious.

He was still watching when a man wearing a faded red shirt left the back door of a building near the saloon, went to a horse carefully hidden in the rear, and mounted. At this distance there was no way of seeing who he was. The man rode strangely. Studying him through the glasses—a relic of Sabre's military years—Matt suddenly realized why the rider seemed strange. He was riding Eastern fashion!

This was no Westerner, slouched and lazy in the saddle, nor yet sitting upright as a cavalryman might. This man rode forward on his horse, a poor practice for the hard miles of desert or mountain riding. Yet it was his surreptitious manner rather than his riding style that intrigued Matt. It required but a few minutes for Matt to see that the route the rider was taking away from town would bring him by near the base of the promontory where he watched.

Reluctant as he was to give over watching the saddled horses, Sabre was sure this strange rider held some clue to his problems. Sliding back on his belly well into the brush, Matt got to his feet and descended the steep trail and took up his place among the boulders beside the trail.

It was very hot here out of the breeze, yet he had waited only a minute until he heard the sound of the approaching horse. He cleared his gun from its holster and moved to the very edge of the road. Then the rider appeared. It was Keys.

Matt's gun stopped him. "Where you ridin', Keys?" Matt asked quietly. "What's this all about?"

"I'm riding to intercept the marshal," Keys said sincerely. "McCarran and Reed plan to send out a posse of their own men to hunt you, then under cover of capturing you, they intend to take the Pivotrock and hold it."

Sabre nodded. That would be it, of course, and he should have guessed it before. "What about the marshal? They'll run into him on the trail."

"No, they're going to swing south of his trail.

They know how he's riding because Reed is guiding him.''

"What's your stake in this? Why ride all the way out there to tell the marshal?"

"It's because of Jenny Curtin," he said frankly. "She's a fine girl, and Bill was a good boy. Both of them treated me fine, as their father did before them. It's little enough to do, and I know too much about the plotting of that devil McCarran."

"Then it is McCarran. Where does Reed stand in this?"

"He's stupid!" Keys said contemptuously. "McCarran is using him and he hasn't the wit to see it. He believes they are partners, but Prince will get rid of him like he does anyone who gets in his way. He'll be rid of Trumbull, too."

"And Sikes?"

"Perhaps. Sikes is a good tool, to a point."

Matt Sabre shoved his hat back on his head. "Keys," he said suddenly, "I want you to have a little faith in me. Believe me, I'm doing what I can to help Jenny Curtin. I did kill her husband, but he was a total stranger who was edgy and started a fight.

"I'd no way of knowing who or what he was, and the gun of a stranger kills as easy as the gun of a known man. But he trusted me. He asked me to come here, to bring his wife five thousand and to help her."

"Five thousand?" Keys stared. "Where did he get that amount of money?"

"I'd like to know," Sabre admitted. Another idea occurred to him. "Keys, you know more about what's going on in this town than anyone else. What do you know about the Sonoma Grant?"

Keys hesitated, then said slowly: "Sabre, I know very little about that. I think the only one who has the true facts is Prince McCarran. I think he gathered all the available papers on both grants and is sure that no matter what his claim, the Grant cannot be substantiated. Nobody knows but McCarran."

"Then I'll go to McCarran," Sabre replied harshly. "I'm going to straighten this outfit it's the last thing I do."

"You go to McCarran and it will be the last thing you do. The man's deadly. He's smooth-talking and treacherous. And then there's Sikes."

"Yes," Sabre admitted. "There's Sikes."

He studied the situation, then looked up. "Look, don't you bother the Marshal. Leave him to me. Every man he's got with him is an enemy to Jenny Curtin, and they would never let you talk. You circle them and ride on to Pivotrock. You tell Camp Gordon what's happening. Tell him of this outfit that's saddled up. I'll do my job here, and then I'll start back."

Long after Keys had departed, Sabre watched. Evidently the posse was awaiting some word from Reed. Would McCarran ride with them? He was too careful. He would wait in Yellowjacket. He would be, as always, an innocent bystander. . . .

Keys, riding up the trail some miles distant, drew up suddenly. He had forgotten to tell Sabre of Prince McCarran's plan to have Sid Trumbull cut him down when he tangled with Sikes. For a long moment Keys sat his horse, staring worriedly and scowling. To go back now would lose time; moreover, there was small chance that Sabre would be there. Matt Sabre would have to take his own chances.

Regretfully, Keys pushed on into the rough country ahead. . . .

Tony Sikes found McCarran seated in the back room at the saloon. McCarran glanced up quickly as he came in, and then nodded.

"Glad to see you, Sikes. I want you close by. I think we'll have visitors today or tomorrow."

"Visitors?" Sikes searched McCarran's face.

"A visitor, I should say. I think we'll see Matt Sabre."

Tony Sikes considered that, turning it over in his mind. Yes, Prince was right. Sabre would not surrender. It would be like him to head for town, hunting Reed. Aside from three or four men, nobody knew of McCarran's connection with the Pivotrock affair. Reed or Trumbull were fronting for him.

Trumbull, Reed and Sikes and Keys. Keys was a shrewd man. He might be a drunk and a piano player, but he had a head on his shoulders.

Sikes' mind leaped suddenly. Keys was not around. This was the first time in weeks that he had not encountered Keys in the bar.

Keys was gone.

Where would he go—to warn Jenny Curtin of the posse? So what? He had nothing against Jenny Curtin. He was a man who fought for hire. Maybe he was on the wrong side in this. Even as he thought of that, he remembered Matt Sabre. The man was sharp as a steel blade, trim, fast. Now that it had been recalled to his mind, he remembered all that he had heard of him as Marshal of Mobeetie.

There was in Tony Sikes a drive that forbade him to admit any man was his fighting superior. Sabre's draw against Trumbull was still the talk of the town—talk that irked Sikes, for folks were beginning to compare the two of them. Many thought Sabre might be faster. That rankled.

He would meet Sabre first, and then drift.

"Don't you think he'll get here?" McCarran asked, looking up at Tony.

Sikes nodded. "He'll get here, all right. He thinks too fast for Trumbull or Reed. Even for that marshal."

Sikes would have Sabre to himself. Sid Trumbull was out of town. Tony Sikes wanted to do his own killing.

Matt Sabre watched the saddled horses. He had that quality of patience so long associated with the

Indian. He knew how to wait, and how to relax. He waited now, letting all his muscles rest. With all his old alertness for danger, his sixth sense that warned him of climaxes, and he knew this situation had reached the explosion point.

The marshal would be returning. Reed and Trumbull would be sure that he did not encounter the posse. And that body of riders, most of whom were henchmen or cronies of Galusha Reed, would sweep down on the Pivotrock and capture it, killing all who were there under the pretense of searching for Matt Sabre.

Keys would warn them, and in time. Once they knew of the danger, Camp Gordon and the others would be wise enough to take the necessary precautions. The marshal was one tentacle, but here in Yellowjacket was the heart of the trouble.

If Prince McCarran and Tony Sikes were removed, the tentacles would shrivel and die. Despite the danger out at Pivotrock, high behind the Mogollon Rim, the decisive blow must be struck right here in Yellowjacket.

He rolled over on his stomach and lifted the glasses. Men were coming from the Yellowjacket Saloon and mounting up. Lying at his ease, he watched them go. There were at least thirty, possibly more. When they had gone he got to his feet and brushed off his clothes. Then he walked slowly down to his horse and mounted.

He rode quietly, one hand lying on his thigh,

his eyes alert, his brain relaxed and ready for impressions.

Marshal Rafe Collins was a just man. He was a frontiersman, a man who knew the West and the men it bred. He was no fool. Shrewd and careful, rigid in his enforcement of the law, yet wise in the ways of men. Moreover, he was Southern in the oldest of Southern traditions, and being so, he understood what Matt Sabre meant when he said it was because he had killed her husband that he must protect Jenny Curtin.

Matt Sabre left his horse at the livery stable. Simpson looked up sharply when he saw him.

"You better watch yourself," he warned. "The whole country's after you, an' they are huntin' blood!"

"I know. What about Sikes? Is he in town?"

"Sure! He never leaves McCarran." Simpson searched his face. "Sikes is no man to tangle with, Sabre. He's chain lightin'."

"I know." Sabre watched his horse led into a shadowed stall. Then he turned to Simpson. "You've been friendly, Simpson. I like that. After today there's goin' to be a new order of things around here, but today I could use some help. What do you know about the Pivotrock deal?"

The man hesitated, chewing slowly. Finally he spat and looked up. "There was nobody to tell until now," he said, "but two things I know. That grant was Curtin's all right, an' he wasn't killed by accident. He was murdered."

"Murdered?"

"Yeah." Simpson's expression was wry. "Like you he liked fancy drinkin' liquor when he could get it. McCarran was right friendly. He asked Curtin to have a drink with him that day, an' Curtin did.

"On'y a few minutes after that he came in here an' got a team to drive back, leavin' his horse in here because it had gone lame. I watched him climb into that rig, an' he missed the step an' almost fell on his face. Then he finally managed to climb in."

"Drunk?" Sabre's eyes were alert and interested.

"Him?" Simpson snorted. "That old coot could stow away more liquor than a turkey could corn. He had only *one* drink, yet he could hardly walk."

"Doped, then?" Sabre nodded. That sounded like McCarran. "And then what?"

"When the team was brought back after they ran away with him, an' after Curtin was found dead, I found a bullet graze on the hip of one of those broncs."

So that was how it had been. A doped man, a skittish team of horses, and a bullet to burn the horse just enough to start it running. Prince McCarran was a thorough man.

"You said you knew that Curtin really owned that grant. How?"

Simpson shrugged. "Because he had that other claim investigated. He must have heard rumors of trouble. There'd been no talk of it that I heard, an' here a man hears everythin'!

"Anyway, he had all the papers with him when he started back to the ranch that day. He showed 'em to me earlier. All the proof."

"And he was murdered that day? Who found the body?"

"Sid Trumbull. He was ridin' that way, sort of accidental-like."

The proof Jenny needed was in the hands of Prince McCarran. By all means, he must call on Prince.

CHAPTER SIX

"Stand Up—and Die!"

Matt Sabre walked to the door and stood there, waiting a monent in the shadow before emerging into the sunlight.

The street was dusty and curiously empty. The rough-fronted gray buildings of unpainted lumber or sand-colored adobe faced him blankly from across and up the street. The hitch rail was deserted, the water trough overflowed a little, making a darkening stain under one end.

Somewhere up the street but behind the buildings a hen began proclaiming her egg to the hemispheres. A single white cloud hung lazily in the blue sky. Matt stepped out. Hitching his gun belts a little, he looked up the street.

Sikes would be in the Yellowjacket. To see

McCarran, he must see Sikes first. That was the way he wanted it. One thing at a time.

He was curiously quiet. He thought of other times when he had faced such situations—of Mobeetie, of that first day out on the plains hunting buffalo, the first time he had killed a man, of a charge the Riffs made on a small desert patrol out of Taudeni long ago.

A faint breeze stirred an old sack that lay near the boardwalk, and further up the street near the water trough, a long gray rat slipped out from under a store and headed toward the drip of water from the trough. Matt Sabre started to walk, moving up the street.

It was not far, as distance goes, but there is no walk so long as the gunman's walk, no pause so long as the pause before gunfire. On this day Sikes would know, instantly, what his presence here presaged. McCarran would know too.

Prince McCarran was not a gambler. He would scarcely trust all to Tony Sikes, no matter how confident he might be. It always paid to have something to back up a facing card. Trust Prince to keep his hole card well covered. But on this occasion he would not be bluffing. He would have a hole card, but where? How? What? And when?

The last was not hard. When—the moment of the gun battle.

He had walked no more than thirty yards when a door creaked and a man stepped into the street. He did not look down toward Sabre, but walked briskly to the center of the street, then faced about sharply like a man on a parade ground.

Tony Sikes.

He wore this day a faded blue shirt that stretched tight over his broad, bony shoulders and fell slack in front where his chest was hollow and his stomach flat. It was too far yet to see his eyes, but Matt Sabre knew what they looked like.

The thin, angular face, the mustache, the high cheek bones and the long, restless fingers. The man's hips were narrow, and there was little enough to his body. Tony Sikes lifted his eyes and stared down the street. His lips were dry, but he felt ready. There was a curious lightness within him, but he liked it so, and he liked the setup. At that moment he felt almost an affection for Sabre.

The man knew so well the rules of the game. He was coming as he should come, and there was something about him—an edged quality, a poised and alert strength.

No sound penetrated the clear globe of stillness. The warm air hung still, with even the wind poised, arrested by the drama in the street. Matt Sabre felt a slow trickle of sweat start from under his hat band. He walked carefully, putting each foot down with care and distinction of purpose. It was Tony Sikes who stopped first, some sixty yards away.

"Well, Matt, here it is. We both knew it was coming."

"Sure." Matt paused too, feet wide apart, hands

swinging wide. "You tied up with the wrong outfit,
Sikes."

"We'd have met, anyway," Sikes looked along
the street at the tall man standing there, looked and
saw his bronzed face, hard and ready. It was not in
Sikes to feel fear of a man with guns. Yet this was
how he would die. It was in the cards. He smiled
suddenly. Yes, he would die by the gun—but not
now.

His hands stirred, and as if their movement was a
signal to his muscles, they flashed in a draw. Before him the dark, tall figure flashed suddenly. It
was no more than that, a blur of movement and a
lifted gun, a movement suddenly stilled, and the
black sullen muzzle of a sixgun that steadied on
him even as he cleared his gun from his open top
holster.

He had been beaten—*beaten to the draw.*

The shock of it triggered Sikes' gun, and he
knew even as the gun bucked in his hand that he
had missed, and then suddenly, Matt Sabre was
running! Running toward him, gun lifted, but not
firing!

In a panic, Sikes saw the distance closing and
he fired as fast as he could pull the trigger, three
times in a thundering cascade of sound. And even
as the hammer fell for the fourth shot, he heard
another gun bellow.

But where? There had been no stab of flame
from Sabre's gun. Sabre was running, a rapidly

moving target, and Sikes had fired too fast, upset by the sudden rush, by the panic of realizing he had been beaten to the draw.

He lifted his right hand gun, dropped the muzzle in a careful arc, and saw Sabre's skull over the barrel. Then Sabre skidded to a halt and his gun hammered bullets.

Flame leaped from the muzzle, stabbing at Sikes, burning him along the side, making his body twitch and the bullet go wild. He switched guns and then something slugged him in the wind and the next he knew he was on the ground.

Matt Sabre had heard that strange shot, but that was another thing. He could not wait now, he could not turn his attention. He saw Sikes go down, but only to his knees, and the gunman had five bullets and the range now was only fifteen yards.

Sikes' gun swung up and Matt fired again. Sikes lunged to his feet, and then his features writhed with agony and breathlessness, and he went down, hard to the ground, twisting in the dust.

Then another bullet bellowed, and a shot kicked up dust at his feet. Matt swung his gun and blasted at an open window, then started for the saloon door. He stopped, hearing a loud cry behind him.

"*Matt*! Sabre?"

It was Sikes, his eyes flared wide. Sabre hesitated, glanced swiftly around, then dropped to his knees in the silent street.

"What is it, Tony? Anything I can do for you?"

"Behind—behind—the desk—you—you—" His faltering voice faded, then strength seemed to flood back and he looked up. "Good man! Too—too fast!"

And then he was dead, gone just like that, and Matt Sabre was striding into the Yellowjacket.

The upstairs room was empty; the stairs were empty; there was no one in sight. Only Hobbs stood behind the bar when he came down. Hobbs, his face set and pale.

Sabre looked at him, eyes steady and cold. "Who came down those stairs?"

Hobbs licked his lips. He choked, then whispered hoarsely. "Nobody—but there's—there's a back stairs."

Sabre wheeled and walked back in quick strides, thumbing shells into his gun. The office door was open and Prince McCarran looked up as he framed himself in the door.

He was writing, and the desk was rumpled with papers, the desk of a busy man. Nearby was a bottle and a full glass.

McCarran lay down his pen. "So? You beat him? I thought you might."

"Did you?" Sabre's gaze was cold. If this man had been running, as he must have run, he gave no evidence of it now. "You should hire them faster, Prince."

"Well," McCarran shrugged, "he was fast

enough until now. But this wasn't my job, anyway. He was workin' for Reed.''

Sabre took a step inside the door, away from the wall, keeping his hands free. His eyes were on those of Prince McCarran, and the Prince watched him, alert, interested.

"That won't ride with me," Matt said. "Reed's a stooge, a perfect stooge. He'll be lucky if he comes back alive from this trip. A lot of that posse you sent out won't come back, either.''

McCarran's eyelids tightened at the mention of the posse. "Forget it," he waved his hand. "Sit down and have a drink. After all, we're not fools, Sabre. We're grown men, and we can talk. I never liked killing, anyway.''

"Unless you do it, or have it done." Sabre's hands remained where they were. "What's the matter, Prince? Yellow? Afraid to do your own killin'?''

McCarran's face was still and his eyes were wide now. "You shouldn't have said that. You shouldn't have called me yellow.''

"Then get on your feet. I hate to shoot a sittin' man.''

"Have a drink and let's talk.''

"Sure." Sabre was elaborately casual. "You have one, too." He reached his hand for the glass that had already been poured, but McCarran's eyes were steady. Sabre switched his hand and grasped the other glass, and then, like a striking snake,

Prince McCarran grasped his right hand and jerked him forward, off-balance.

At the same time, McCarran's left flashed back to the holster high on his left side, butt forward, and the gun jerked up and free. Matt Sabre, instead of trying to jerk his right hand free, let his weight go forward, following and hurling himself against McCarran. The chair went over with a crash and Prince tried to straighten, but Matt was riding him back. He crashed into the wall and Sabre broke free.

Prince swung his gun up, and Sabre's left palm slapped down, knocking the gun aside and gripping the hand across the thumb. His right hand came up under the gun barrel, twisting it back over and out of McCarran's hands. Then he shoved him back and dropped the gun, slapping him across the mouth with his open palm.

It was a free swing and it cracked like a pistol shot. McCarran's face went white from the blow and he rushed, swinging, but Sabre brought up his knee in the charging man's groin. Then, he smashed him in the face with his elbow, pushing him over and back. McCarran dove past him, blood streaming from his crushed nose, and grabbed wildly at the papers. His hand came up with a bulldog .41.

Matt saw the hand shoot for the papers and even as the .41 appeared his own gun was lifting. He fired first, three times, at a range of four feet.

Prince McCarran stiffened, lifted to his tiptoes,

then plunged over on his face and lay still among the litter of papers and broken glass.

Sabre swayed drunkenly. He recalled what Sikes had said about the desk. He caught the edge and jerked it aside, swinging the desk away from the wall. Behind it was a small panel with a knob. It was locked, but a bullet smashed the lock. He jerked it open. A thick wad of bills, a small sack of gold coins, a sheaf of papers.

A glance sufficed. These were the papers Simpson had mentioned. The thick parchment of the original grant, the information on the conflicting Sonoma grant, and then . . . He glanced swiftly through them, then at a pound of horses' hoofs, he stuffed them inside his shirt. He stopped, stared. His shirt was soaked with blood.

Fumbling, he got the papers into his pocket, then stared down at himself. Sikes had hit him. Funny, he had never felt it. Only a shock, a numbness. Now Reed was coming back.

Catching up a sawed-off express shotgun, he started for the door, weaving like a drunken man. He never even got to the door.

The sound of galloping horses was all he could hear—galloping horses, and then a faint smell of something that reminded him of a time he had been wounded in North Africa. His eyes flickered open and the first thing he saw was a room's wall with the picture of a man with mutton chop whiskers and spectacles.

He turned his head and saw Jenny Curtin watching him. "So? You've decided to wake up. You're getting lazy, Matt. Mr. Sabre. On the ranch you always were the first one up."

He stared at her. She had never looked half so charming, and that was bad. It was bad because it was time to be out of here and on a horse.

"How long have I been here?"

"Only about a day and a half. You lost a lot of blood."

"What happened at the ranch? Did Keys get there in time?"

"Yes, and I stayed. The others left right away."

"You *stayed*?"

"The others," she said quietly, "went down the road about two miles. There was Camp Gordon, Tom Judson, Pepito and Keys. And Rado, of course. They went down the road while I stood out in the ranchyard and let them see me. The boys ambushed them."

"Was it much of a fight?"

"None at all. The surprise was so great that they broke and ran. Only three weren't able, and four were badly wounded."

"You found the papers? Including the one about McCarran sending the five thousand in marked bills to El Paso?"

"Yes," she said simply. "We found that. He planned on having Billy arrested and charged with theft. He planned that, and then if he got killed, so much the better. It was only you he didn't count on."

"No," Matt Sabre stared at his hands, strangely white now. "He didn't count on me."

So it was all over now. She had her ranch, she was a free woman, and people would leave her alone. There was only one thing left. He had to tell her. To tell her that he was the one who had killed her husband.

He turned his head on the pillow. "One thing more," he began. "I—"

"Not now. You need rest."

"Wait. I have to tell you this. It's about—about Billy."

"You mean that you—you were the one who—?"

"Yes, I—" he hesitated, reluctant at last to say it.

"I know. I know you did, Matt. I've known from the beginning, even without all the things you said."

"I talked when I was delirious?"

"A little. But I knew, Matt. Call it intuition, anything you like, but I knew. You see, you told me how his eyes were when he was drawing his gun. Who could have known that but the man who shot him?"

"I see." His face was white. "Then I'd better rest. I've got some travelling to do."

She was standing beside him. "Travelling? Do you have to go on, Matt? From all you said last night, I thought—I thought—" her face flushed—

"maybe you—didn't want to travel any more. Stay with us, Matt, if you want to. We would like to have you, and Billy's been asking for you. He wants to know where his spurs are."

After awhile, he admitted carefully, "Well, I guess I should stay and see that he gets them. A fellow should always make good on his promises to kids, I reckon."

"You'll stay then? You won't leave?"

Matt stared up at her. "I reckon," he said quietly, "I'll never leave unless you send me away."

She smiled and touched his hair. "Then you'll be here a long time, Mathurin Sabre, a very long time."

THE BLACK ROCK
COFFIN-MAKERS

CHAPTER ONE

Five Thousand Dollar Fake

Jim Gatlin had been up the creek and over the mountains, and more than once had been on both ends of a six-shooter. Lean and tall, with shoulders wide for his height and a face like saddle leather, he was, at the moment, doing a workmanlike job of demolishing the last of a thick steak and picking off isolated beans that had escaped his initial attack. He was a thousand miles from home and knew nobody in the town of Tucker.

He glanced up as the door opened and saw a short, thick-bodied man. The man gave one startled look at Jim and ducked back out of sight. Gatlin blinked in surprise, then shrugged and filled his coffee cup from the pot standing on the restaurant table.

Puzzled, he listened to the rapidly receding pound of a horse's hoofs, then rolled a smoke, sitting back with a contented sigh. Two hundred and fifty odd miles to the north was the herd he had drifted northwest from Texas. The money the critters had brought was in the belt around his waist, and his pants' pockets. Nothing remained now but to return to Texas, bank the profit and pick up a new herd.

The outer door opened again and a tall girl entered the restaurant. Turning right, she started for the door leading to the hotel. She stopped abruptly as though his presence had only then registered. She turned, and her eyes widened in alarm. Swiftly she crossed the room to him. "Are you insane?" she whispered. "Sitting here like that when the town is full of Wing Cary's hands? They know you're coming and have been watching for you for days!"

Gatlin looked up, smiling. "Ma'am, you've sure got the wrong man, although if a girl as purty as you is worried about him, he sure is a lucky fellow. I'm a stranger here. I never saw the place until an hour ago!"

She stepped back, puzzled, and then the door slammed open once more and a man stepped into the room. He was as tall as Jim, but thinner, and his dark eyes were angry. "Get away from him, Lisa! I'm killin' him—right now!"

The man's hand flashed for a gun, and Gatlin dove sidewise to the floor, drawing as he fell. A gun roared in the room, then Gatlin fired twice.

The tall man caught himself, jerking his left arm against his ribs, his face twisted as he gasped for breath. Then he wilted slowly to the floor, his gun sliding from his fingers.

Gatlin got to his feet, staring at the stranger. He swung his eyes to the girl staring at him. "Who is that hombre?" he snapped. "What's this all about? Who did he think I was?"

"You—you're not—you aren't Jim Walker?" Her voice was high, amazed.

"Walker?" He shook his head. "I'm sure as hell not. The name is Gatlin. I'm just driftin' through."

There was a rush of feet in the street outside. She caught his hand. "Come! Come quickly! They won't listen to you! They'll kill you! All the Cary outfit are in town!"

She ran beside him, dodging into the hotel, and then swiftly down a hall. As the front door burst open, they plunged out the back and into the alley behind the building. Unerringly, she led him to the left, and then opened the back door of another building and drew him inside. Silently she closed the door and stood close beside him, panting in the darkness.

Shouts and curses rang from the building next door. A door banged, and men charged up and down outside. Jim was still holding his gun, but now he withdrew the empty shells and fed two into the cylinder to replace those fired. He slipped a sixth into the usually empty chamber. "What is this place?" he whispered. "Will they come here?"

"It's a law office," she whispered. "I work here part time, and I left the door open myself. They'll not think of this place." Stealthily, she lifted the bar and dropped it into place. "Better sit down. They'll be searching the streets for some time."

He found the desk and seated himself on the corner, well out of line with the windows. He could see only the vaguest outline of her face. She was, he remembered, pretty. The gray eyes were wide and clear, her figure rounded yet slim. "What is this?" he repeated. "What was he gunnin' for me for?"

"It wasn't you. He thought you were Jim Walker, of the XY. If you aren't actually him you look enough like him to be a brother, a twin brother."

"Where is he? What goes on here? Who was that hombre who tried to gun me?"

She paused, and seemed to be thinking, and he had the idea she was still uncertain whether to believe him or not. "The man you killed was Bill Trout. He was the bad man of Paradise country and segundo on Wing Cary's Flying C spread. Walker called him a thief and a murderer in talking to Cary, and Trout threatened to shoot him on sight. Walker hasn't been seen since, and that was four days ago, so everybody believed Walker had skipped the country. Nobody blamed him much."

"What's it all about?" Gatlin inquired.

"North of here, up beyond Black Rock, is Alder Creek country, with some rich bottom hayland lying in several corners of the mountains. This is dry country, but that Alder Creek area has springs and some small streams flowing down out of the hills. The streams flow into the desert and die there, so the water is good only for the man who controls the range."

"And that was Walker?"

"No, up until three weeks ago it was old Dave Butler. Then Dave was thrown from his horse and killed, and when they read his will, he had left the property to be sold at auction and the money paid to his nephew and niece back in New York. However, the joker was, he stipulated that Jim Walker was to get the ranch if he would bid ten thousand cash and forty thousand on his note, payable in six years."

"In other words, he wanted Walker to have the property?" Jim asked. "He got first chance at it?"

"That's right. And I was to get second chance. If Jim didn't want to make the bid, I could have it for the same price. If neither of us wanted it, the ranch was to go on public auction, and that means that Cary and Horwick would get it. They have the money, and nobody around here could outbid them."

The street outside was growing quieter as the excitement of the chase died down. "I think," Lisa continued, "that Uncle Dave wanted Jim to have the property because Jim did so much to develop it. Jim was foreman of the XY acting for Dave. Then, Uncle Dave knew my father and liked me, and he knew I loved the ranch, so he wanted me to have second chance, but I don't have the money, and they all know it. Jim had some of it, and he could get the rest. I think that was the real trouble behind his trouble with Trout. I believe Wing deliberately set Trout to kill him, and Jim's statements about Bill were a result of the pushing around Bill Trout had given him."

The pattern was not unfamiliar, and Gatlin could easily appreciate the situation. Water was gold in this country of sparse grass. To a cattleman, such a ranch as Lisa described could be second to none, with plenty of water and grass and good hay meadows. Suddenly she caught his arm. Men were talking outside the door.

"Looks like he got plumb away, Wing. Old Ben swears there was nobody in the room with him but that Lisa Cochrane, an' she never threw that gun, but how Jim Walker ever beat Trout is more'n I can see. Why, Bill was the fastest man around here unless it's you or me."

"That wasn't Walker, Pete. It couldn't have been!"

"Ben swears it was, an' Woody Hammer busted right through the door in front of him. Said it was Jim, all right."

Wing Cary's voice was irritable. "I tell you, it couldn't have been!" he flared. "Jim Walker never saw the day he dared face Trout with a gun,'' he added. ''I've seen Walker draw an' he never was fast.''

''Maybe he wasn't,'' Pete Chasin agreed dryly, ''but Trout's dead, ain't he?''

''Three days left,'' Cary mused. ''Lisa Cochrane hasn't the money, and it doesn't look like Walker will even be bidding. Let it ride, Pete, I don't think we need to worry about anything. Even if that was Walker, an' I'd take an oath it wasn't, he's gone for good now. All we have to do is sit tight.''

The two moved off, and Jim Gatlin, staring at the girl in the semi-darkness, saw her lips were pressed tight. His eyes had grown accustomed to the dim light, and he could see around the small office. It was a simple room with a desk, chair and filing cabinets. Well-filled bookcases lined the walls.

He got to his feet. ''I've got to get my gear out of that hotel,'' he said, ''and my horse.''

''You're leaving?'' she asked.

Jim glanced at her in surprise. ''Why, sure! Why stay here in a fight that's not my own? I've already killed one man, and if I stay I'll have to kill more or be killed myself. There's nothing here for me.''

''Did you notice something?'' she asked suddenly. ''Wing Cary seemed very sure that Jim Walker wasn't coming back, that you weren't he.''

Gatlin frowned. He had noticed it, and it had him wondering. ''He did sound mighty sure. Like he might *know* he wasn't coming back.''

They were silent in the dark office, yet each knew what the other was thinking. Jim Walker was dead. Pete Chasin had not known it. Neither, obviously, had Bill Trout.

"What happens to you then?" Gatlin asked suddenly. "You lose the ranch?"

She shrugged. "I never had it, and never really thought I would have it, only . . . well, if Jim had lived . . . I mean, if Jim got the ranch we'd have made out. We were very close, like brother and sister. Now, I don't know what I can do."

"You haven't any people?"

"None that I know of." Her head came up suddenly. "Oh, it isn't myself I'm thinking of, it's all the old hands, the ranch itself. Uncle Dave hated Cary, and so do his men. Now he'll get the ranch and they'll all be fired, and he'll ruin the place! That what he's wanted all along."

Gatlin shifted his feet. "Tough," he said, "mighty tough."

He opened the door slightly. "Thanks," he said, "for getting me out of there." She didn't reply, so after a moment he stepped out of the door and drew it gently to behind him.

There was no time to lose. He must be out of town by daylight and with miles behind him. There was no sense getting mixed up in somebody else's fight, for all he'd get out of it would be a bellyful of lead. There was nothing he could do to help. He moved swiftly, and within a matter of minutes was in his hotel room. Apparently, searching for Jim

Walker, they hadn't considered his room in the hotel, so Gatlin got his duffle together, stuffed it into his saddlebags and picked up his rifle. With utmost care he eased down the back stairs and into the alley.

The streets were once more dark and still. What had become of the Flying C hands, he didn't know, but none were visible. Staying on back streets, he made his way carefully to the livery barn, but here his chance of cover grew less, for he must enter the wide door with a light glowing over it.

After listening, he stepped out and, head down, walked through the door. Turning, he hurried to the stall where his powerful black waited. It was the work of only a few minutes to saddle up. He led the horse out of the stall and caught up the bridle. With a hand on the pommel a voice stopped him.

"Lightin' out?"

It was Pete Chasin's voice. Slowly he released his grip on the pommel and turned slightly. The man was hidden in a stall. "Why not?" Gatlin asked. "I'm not goin' to be a shootin' gallery for nobody. This ain't my range, an' I'm slopin' out of here for Texas. I'm no trouble hunter."

He heard Chasin's chuckle. "Don't reckon you are. But it seems a shame not to make the most of your chance. What if I offered you five thousand to stay? Five thousand, in cash?"

"Five thousand?" Gatlin blinked. That was half as much as he had in his belt, and the ten thousand he carried had taken much hard work and bargaining to get. Buying a herd, chancing the long drive.

"What would I have to do?" he demanded.

Chasin came out of the stall. "Be yourself," he said, "just be yourself—but let folks think you're Jim Walker. Then you buy a ranch here . . . I'll give yuh the money, an' then yuh hit the trail."

Chasin was trying to double-cross Cary! To get the ranch for himself!

Gatlin hesitated, "That's a lot of money, but these boys toss a lot of lead. I might not live to spend the dough."

"I'll hide yuh out." Chasin argued. "I've got a cabin in the hills. I'd hide yuh out with four, five of my boys to stand guard. Yuh'd be safe enough. Then yuh could come down, put your money on the line an' sign the papers."

"Suppose they want Walker's signature checked?"

"Jim Walker never signed more'n three, four papers in his life. He left no signatures hereabouts. I've took pains to be sure."

Five thousand because he looked like a man. It was easy money, and he'd be throwing a monkey wrench into Wing Cary's plans. Cary, a man he'd decided he disliked. "Sounds like a deal," he said. "Let's go!"

The cabin on the north slope of Bartlett Peak was well hidden, and there was plenty of grub. Pete Chasin left him there with two men to guard him, and two more standing by on the trail toward town. All through the following day, Jim Gatlin loafed, smoking cigarettes and talking idly with the two men. Hab Johnson was a big, unshaven hombre with a sullen face and a surly manner. He talked little, and then only to growl. Pink Stabineau was a wide-chested, flat-faced jasper with an agreeable grin.

Gatlin had a clear idea of his own situation. He could use five thousand, but he knew Chasin never intended him to leave the country with it, and doubted if he would last an hour after the ranch was transferred to Chasin himself. Yet Gatlin had been around the rough country and he knew a trick or two of his own. Several times he thought of Lisa Cochrane, but avoided that angle as much as he could.

After all, she had no chance to get the ranch, and Walker was probably dead. That left it between Cary and Chasin. The unknown Horwick of whom he had heard mention was around, too, but he seemed to stand with Cary in everything. Yet he was restless and irritable, and he kept remembering the girl beside him in the darkness, and her regrets at breaking up the old outfit. Jim Gatlin had been a hand who rode for the brand; he knew what it meant to have a ranch sold out from under a bunch of old hands. The home that had been theirs gone, the friends drifting apart never to meet again, everything changed.

He finished breakfast on the morning of the

second day, then walked out of the cabin with his
saddle. Hab Johnson looked up sharply. "Where
yuh goin'?" he demanded.

"Ridin'," Gatlin said briefly, "an' don't worry.
I'll be back."

Johnson chewed a stem of grass, his hard eyes
on Jim's. "Yuh ain't goin' nowheres. The boss
said to watch yuh an' keep yuh here. Here yuh
stay."

Gatlin dropped his saddle. "You aren't keepin' me
nowheres, Hab," he said flatly. "I've had enough
sittin' around. I aim to see a little of this country."

"I reckon not." Hab got to his feet. "Yuh may
be a fast hand with a gun, but yuh ain't gittin' both
of us, nor yuh ain't so foolish as to try." He
waved a big hand. "Now yuh go back an' set
down."

"I started for a ride," Jim said quietly, "an' a
ride I'm takin'." He stooped to pick up the saddle
and saw Hab's boots as the big man started for
him. Jim had lifted the saddle clear of the ground,
and now he hurled it, suddenly, in Hab's path.
The big man stumbled and hit the ground on his
hands and knees, then started up.

As he came up half way, Jim slugged him. Hab
tottered, fighting for balance, and Gatlin moved
in, striking swiftly with a volley of lefts and rights
to the head. Hab went down and hit hard, then
came up with a lunge, but Gatlin dropped him

again. Blood dripped from smashed lips and a cut on his cheekbone.

Gatlin stepped back, working his fingers. His hard eyes flicked to Pink Stabineau, who was smoking quietly, resting on one elbow, looking faintly amused. "You stoppin' me?" Gatlin demanded.

Pink grinned. "Me? Now where did yuh get an idea like that? Take your ride. Hab's just too pernickety about things. Anyway, he's always wantin' to slug somebody. Now maybe he'll be quiet for a spell."

There was a dim trail running northwest from the cabin and Gatlin took it, letting his horse choose his own gait. The black was a powerful animal, not only good on a trail but an excellent roping horse and he moved out eagerly, liking the new country. When he had gone scarcely more than two miles, he skirted the edge of a high meadow with plenty of grass, then left the trail and turned off along a bench of the mountain, riding due north.

Suddenly the mountain fell away before him, and below in a long finger of grass he saw the silver line of a creek, and nestled against a shoulder of the mountain he discerned roofs among the trees. Pausing, Jim rolled a smoke and studied the lie of the land. Northward, for all of ten miles, there was good range. Dry, but not so bad as over the mountain, and in the spring and early summer it would be good grazing land. He had looked at too much range not to detect, from the colors of the valley before him, some of the varieties of grass and brush. Northwest the range stretched away through a wide gap in the mountains, and he seemed to distinguish a deeper green in the distance.

Old Dave Butler had chosen well, and his XY had, Gatlin could see as he rode nearer, been well handled. Tanks had been built to catch some of the overflow from the mountains and to prevent the washing of valuable range. The old man, and evidently Jim Walker, had worked hard to build this ranch into something. Even while wanting money for his relatives in the east, Butler had tried to insure that the work would be continued after his death. Walker would continue it, and so would Lisa Cochrane.

CHAPTER TWO

Kill-Branded Pardner

All morning he rode, and well into the afternoon, studying the range but avoiding the buildings. Once, glancing back, he saw a group of horsemen riding swiftly out of the mountains from which he had come and heading for the XY. Reining in, he watched from a vantage point among some huge boulders. Men wouldn't ride that fast without adequate reason . . .

Morosely, he turned and started back along the way he had come, thinking more and more of Lisa. Five thousand was a lot of money, but what he was doing was not dishonest and so far he had played the game straight. Still why think of that? In a few days he'd have the money in his pocket and be headed for Texas. He turned on the brow of

125

the hill and glanced back, carried away despite himself by the beauty of the wide sweep of range.

Pushing on, he skirted around and came toward the cabin from the town trail. He was riding with his mind far away when the black snorted violently and shied. Jim drew up, staring at the man who lay sprawled in the trail. It was the cowhand Pete Chasin had left on guard there. He'd been shot through the stomach and a horse had been ridden over him.

Swinging down, a quick check showed the man was dead. Jim grabbed up the reins and sprang into the saddle. Sliding a sixgun from its holster, he pushed forward, riding cautiously. The tracks told him that a party of twelve horsemen had come this way.

He heard the wind in the trees, the distant cry of an eagle, but nothing more. He rode out into the clearing before the cabin and drew up. Another man had died here. It wasn't Stabineau nor Hab Johnson, but the other guard, who must have retreated to this point for aid.

Gun in hand, Gatlin pushed the door open and looked into the cabin. Everything was smashed, yet when he swung down and went in, he found his own gear intact, under the overturned bed. He threw his bed roll on his horse and loaded up his saddlebags. He jacked a shell into the chamber of the Winchester and was about to mount up when he heard a muffled cry.

Turning, he stared around, then detected a faint

stir among the leaves of a mountain mahogany. Warily he walked over and stepped around the bush.

Pink Stabineau, his face pale, and his shirt dark with blood, lay sprawled on the ground. Curiously there was still a faint touch of humor in his eyes when he looked up at Gatlin. "Got me," he said finally. "It was that damned Hab. He sold us out . . . to Wing Cary. The damn' dirty son!"

Jim dropped to his knees and gently unbuttoned the man's shirt. The wound was low down on the left side and although he seemed to have lost much blood, there was a chance. Working swiftly, he built a fire, heated water and bathed and then dressed the wound. From time to time Pink talked, telling him much of what he suspected, that Cary would hunt Chasin down now, and kill him.

"If they fight," Jim asked, "who'll win?"

Stabineau grinned wryly. "Cary . . . he's tough, an' cold as ice. Pete's too jumpy. He's fast, but mark my words, if they face each other he'll shoot too fast and miss his first shot. Wing won't miss!

"But it won't come to that. Wing's a cinch player. He'll chase him down an' the bunch will gun him to death. Wing's blood-thirsty."

Leaving food and a canteen of water beside the wounded man, and giving him two blankets, Jim Gatlin mounted. His deal was off then. The thought left him with a distinct feeling of relief. He had never liked any part of it, and he found himself without sympathy for Pete Chasin. The man had attempted a double-cross and failed.

Well, the road was open again now, and there was nothing between him and Texas but the miles. Yet he hesitated, and then turned his horse toward the XY. He rode swiftly, and at sundown was at the ranch. He watched it for a time, and saw several hands working around, yet there seemed little activity. No doubt they were waiting to see what was to happen.

Suddenly, a sorrel horse started out from the ranch and swung into the trail toward town. Jim Gatlin squinted his eyes against the fading glare of the sun and saw the rider was a woman. That would be Lisa Cochrane. Suddenly he swung the black and, touching spurs to the horse, raced down the mountains to intercept her.

Until that moment he had been uncertain as to the proper course, but now he knew, yet for all his speed, his eyes were alert and watchful for he realized the risk he ran. Wing Cary would be quick to discover that as long as he was around and alive that there was danger, and even now the rancher might have his men out, scouring the country for him. Certainly, there were plausible reasons enough, for it could be claimed that he had joined with Chasin in a plot to get the ranch by appearing as Jim Walker.

Lisa's eyes widened when she saw him. "I thought you'd be gone by now. There's a posse after you!"

"You mean some of Cary's men?" he corrected.

"I mean a posse. Wing has men on your trail, too, but they lost you somehow. He claims that you were tied up in a plan with Pete Chasin to get the ranch, and that you killed Jim Walker!"

"That *I* did?" his eyes searched her face. "You mean that? He actually claims that?"

She nodded, watching him. "He says that story about your being here was all nonsense, that you actually came on purpose, that you an' Chasin rigged it that way! You'll have to admit it looks funny, you arriving right at this time and looking just like Jim."

"What if it does?" he demanded impatiently. "I never heard of Jim Walker until you mentioned him to me, and I never heard of the town of Tucker until a few hours before I met you."

"You'd best go, then," she warned, "they're all over the country. Sheriff Eaton would take you in, but Wing wouldn't, nor any of his boys. They'll kill you on sight."

"Yeah," he agreed, "I can see that." Nevertheless, he didn't stir, but continued to roll a cigarette. She sat still, watching him curiously. Finally he looked up. "I'm in a fight," he admitted,"and not one I asked for. Cary is making this a mighty personal thing, ma'am, an' I reckon I ain't even figurin' on leavin'." He struck a match. "You got any chance of gettin' the ranch?"

"How could I? I have no money!"

"Supposin'," he suggested, squinting an eye

against the smoke, "you had a pardner—with ten thousand dollars?"

Lisa shook her head. "Things like that don't happen," she said. "They just don't."

"I've got ten thousand dollars on me," Gatlin volunteered, "an' I've been pushed into this whether I like it or not. I say we ride into Tucker now, an' we see this boss of yours, the lawyer. I figure he could get the deal all set up for us tomorrow. Are you game?"

"You—you really have that much?" She looked doubtfully at his shabby range clothes. "It's honest money?"

"I drove cattle to Montana," he said. "That was my piece of it. Let's go."

"Not so fast!" The words rapped out sharply. "I'll take that money, an' take it now! Woody, get that girl!"

For reply Jim slapped the spurs to the black and at the same instant, slapped the sorrel a ringing blow. The horses sprang off together in a dead run! Behind them a rifle shot rang out and Jim felt the bullet clip past his skull. "Keep goin'!" he yelled. "Ride!"

At a dead run they swung down the trail, and then Jim saw a side trail he had noticed on his left. He jerked his head at the girl and grabbed at her bridle. It was too dark to see the gesture, but she felt the tug and turned the sorrel after him, mounting swiftly up the steep side hill under the trees.

Here the soft needles made it impossible for their horses' hoofs to be heard, and Jim led the way, pushing on under the pines.

That it would be only a minute or so before Cary discovered his error was certain, but each minute counted. A wall lifted on their right and they rode on, keeping in the intense darkness close under it, but then another wall appeared on their left and they were boxed in. Behind them they heard a yell, distant now, but indication enough their trail had been found. Boulders and slabs of rock loomed before them, but the black horse turned down a slight incline and worked his way around the rocks. From time to time they spoke to each other to keep together, but he kept moving, knowing that Wing Cary would be close behind.

The canyon walls seemed to be drawing closer and the boulders grew larger and larger. Somewhere Jim heard water running, and the night air was cool and slightly damp on his face. He could smell pines, so knew there were trees about and they had not ridden completely out of them. Yet Jim was becoming worried, for the canyon walls towered above them and obviously there was no break. If this turned out to be a box canyon, they were bottled up. One man could hold this canyon corked with no trouble at all.

The black began to climb and in a few minutes walked out on a flat of grassy land. The moon was rising but as yet there was no light in this deep canyon.

Lisa rode up beside him. "Jim," it was the first time she had ever called him by name, "I'm afraid we're in for it now. Unless I'm mistaken this is a box canyon. I've never been up here, but I've heard of it, and there's no way out."

"I was afraid of that." The black horse stopped as he spoke and he heard water falling ahead. He urged the horse forward but he refused to obey. Jim swung down into the darkness. "Pool," he said. "We'll find some place to hole up and wait for daylight."

They found a group of boulders and seated themselves among them, stripping the saddles from their horses and picketing them on a small patch of grass behind the boulders. Then for a long time they talked, the casual talk of two people finding out about each other. Jim talked of his early life on the Neuces, of his first trip into Mexico after horses when he was fourteen, and how they were attacked by Apaches. There had been three Indian fights that trip, two south of the border and one north of it.

He had no idea when sleep took him, but he awakened with a start to find the sky growing gray, and to see Lisa Cochrane sleeping on the grass six feet away. She looked strangely young with her face relaxed and her lips slightly parted. A dark tendril of hair had blown across her cheek. He turned away and walked out to the horses. The grass was thick and rich here.

He studied their position with care, and found they were on a terrace separated from the end wall of the canyon only by the pool, at least an acre of clear, cold water into which a small fall fell from the cliff above. There were a few trees, and some of the scattered boulders they had encountered the previous night. The canyon on which they had come was a wild jumble of boulders and brush surmounted on either side by cliffs that lifted nearly three hundred feet. While escape might be impossible if Wing Cary attempted, as he surely would, to guard the opening, yet their own position was secure, too, for one man with a rifle might stand off an army from the terrace.

After he had watered the horses he built a fire and put water on for coffee. Seeing some trout in the pool, he tried his luck, and from the enthusiasm with which they went for his bait the pool could never have been fished before, or not in a long time. Lisa came from behind the boulders just as the coffee came to a boil. "What is this, a picnic?" she asked brightly.

He grinned, touching his unshaven jaw. "With this beard?" He studied her a minute. "You'd never guess you'd spent the night on horseback or sleeping at the end of a canyon," he said. Then his eyes sobered. "Can you handle a rifle? I mean, well enough to stand off Cary's boys if they tried to come up here?"

She turned quickly and glanced down the canyon. The nearest boulders to the terrace edge were sixty yards away, and the approach even that close would not be easy. "I think so," she said. "What are you thinking of?"

He gestured at the cliff. "I've been studyin' that. With a mite of luck a man might make it up there."

Her face paled. "It isn't worth it. We're whipped, and we might as well admit it. All we can do now is sit still and wait until the ranch is sold."

"No," he said positively. "I'm goin' out of here if I have to blast my way out. They've made a personal matter out of this, now," he glanced at her, "I sort of have a feeling you should have that ranch. Lookin' at it yesterday I just couldn't imagine it without you. You lived there, didn't you?"

"Most of my life. My folks were friends of Uncle Dave's, and after they were killed I stayed on with him."

"Did he leave you anything?" he asked.

She shook her head. "I . . . I think he expected me to marry Jim . . . he always wanted it that way, but we never felt like that about each other, and yet Jim told me after Uncle Dave died that I was to consider the place my home, if he got it."

As they ate, he listened to her talk while he studied the cliff. It wasn't going to be easy, and yet it could be done.

A shout rang out from the rocks behind them, and they both moved to the boulders, but there was nobody in sight. A voice yelled again that Jim spotted as that of Wing Cary. He shouted a reply, and Wing yelled back, "We'll let Lisa come out if she wants, an' you, too, if you come with your hands up!"

Lisa shook her head, so Gatlin shouted back, "We like it here! Plenty of water, plenty of grub! If you want us you'll have to come an' get us!"

In the silence that followed, Lisa said, "*He* can't stay, not if he attends the auction."

Jim turned swiftly. "Take the rifle. If they start to come, shoot an' shoot to kill! I'm going to take a chance!"

Keeping out of sight behind the worn gray boulders, Gatlin worked his way swiftly along the edge of the pool toward the cliff face. As he felt his way along the rocky edge, he stared down into the water. That pool was deep, from the looks of it. And that was something to remember.

At the cliff face he stared up. It looked even easier than he thought, and at one time and another he had climbed worse faces. However, once he was well up the face he would be within sight of the watchers below . . . or would he?

CHAPTER THREE

Hell's Chimney

He put a hand up and started, working his way to a four-inch ledge that projected from the face of the rock and slanted sharply upward. There were occasional clumps of brush growing from the rock, and they would offer some security. A rifle shot rang out behind him, then a half dozen more, farther off. Lisa had fired at something and had been answered from down the canyon.

The ledge was steep, but there were good handholds and he worked his way along it more swiftly than he would have believed possible. His clothing blended well with the rock, and by refraining from any sudden movements there was a chance that he could make it.

When almost two hundred feet up the face, he

paused, resting on a narrow ledge, partly concealed by an outcropping. He looked up, but the wall was sheer. Beyond there was a chimney, but almost too wide for climbing and the walls looked slick as a blue clay sidehill. Yet study the cliff as he would, he could see no other point where he might climb farther. Worse, part of that chimney was exposed to fire from below.

If they saw him he was through. He'd be stuck, with no chance of evading the fire. Yet he knew he'd take the chance. Squatting on the ledge, he pulled off his boots, and running a loop of piggin' string through their loops, he slung them from his neck. Slipping thongs over his guns, he got into the chimney and braced his back against one side, then lifted his feet, first his left, then his right, against the opposite wall.

Whether Lisa was watching or not, he didn't know, but almost at that instant she began firing. The chimney was, at this point, all of six feet deep, and wide enough to allow for climbing, but very risky climbing. His palms flat against the slippery wall, he began to inch himself upward, working his stocking feet up the opposite wall. Slowly, every movement a danger, his breath coming slow, his eyes riveted on his feet, he began to work his way higher.

Sweat poured down his face and smarted in his eyes, and he could feel it trickling down his stomach under his wool shirt. Before he was halfway up his breath was coming in great gasps and his muscles were weary with the strain of opposing their strength against the walls to keep from falling. Then, miraculously, the chimney narrowed a little, and climbing was easier.

He glanced up. Not over twenty feet to go! His heart bounded and he renewed his effort. A foot slipped, and he felt an agonizing moment when fear throttled him and he seemed about to fall. To fall meant to bound from that ledge and go down, down into that deep green pool at the foot of the cliff, a fall of nearly three hundred feet!

Something smacked against the wall near him and from below there was a shout. Then Lisa opened fire, desperately, he knew, to give him covering fire. Another shot splashed splinters in his face and he struggled wildly, sweat poured from him, to get up those last few feet. Suddenly the rattle of fire ceased, and then opened up again. He risked a quick glance and saw Lisa Cochrane running out in the open, and as she ran, she halted and fired!

She was risking her life, making her death or capture inevitable, to save him!

Suddenly a breath of air was against his cheek and he hunched himself higher, his head reaching the top of the cliff. Another shot rang out and howled off the edge of the rock beside him. Then his hands were on the edge, and he rolled over on solid ground, trembling in every limb.

A moment only, for there was no time to waste.

He got to his feet, staggering, and stared around. He was on the very top of the mountain and Tucker lay far away to the south. He seated himself and got his boots on, then slipped the thongs from his guns. Walking swiftly as his still trembling muscles would allow, he started south.

There was a creek, he remembered, that flowed down into the flatlands from somewhere near here, an intermittent stream, but with a canyon that offered an easy outlet to the plain below. Studying the terrain, he saw a break in the rocky plateau that might be it, and started down the steep mountainside through the cedar, toward that break.

A horse was what he needed most. With a good horse under him he might make it. He had a good lead, for they must come around the mountain, a good ten miles by the quickest trail. That ten miles might get him to town before they could catch him, to town and to the lawyer who would make the bid for them, even if Eaton had him in jail by that time. Suddenly, remembering how Lisa had run out into the open, risking her life to protect him, he realized he would willingly give his own to save her.

He stopped, mopping his face with a handkerchief. The canyon broke away before him and he dropped into it, sliding and climbing to the bottom. When he reached the bottom he started off toward the flat country at a swinging stride. A half hour later, his shirt dark with sweat, the canyon suddenly spread wide into the flat country. Dust hung in the air, and he slowed down, hearing voices.

"Give 'em a blow." It was a man's voice speaking. "Hear any more shootin'?"

"Not me." The second voice was thin and nasal. "Reckon it was my ears mistakin' themselves."

"Let's go, Eaton." another voice said. "It's too hot here. I'm pinin' for some o' that good XY well water!"

Gatlin pushed his way forward. "Hold it, Sheriff! You huntin' me?"

Sheriff Eaton was a tall, gray-haired man with a handlebar mustache and keen blue eyes. "If you're Gatlin, an' from the looks of yuh, yuh must be, I sure am! How come you're so all fired anxious to get caught?"

Gatlin explained swiftly. "That girl's back there, an' they got her!" he finished. "Sheriff, I'd be mighty pleased if yuh'd send a few men after her, or go yourself an' let the rest of them go to Tucker with me."

Eaton studied him. "What you want in Tucker?"

"To bid that ranch in for Lisa Cochrane!" he said flatly. "Sheriff, that girl saved my bacon back there, an' I'm a grateful man! You get me to town to get that money in Lawyer Ashton's hands, an' I'll go to jail!"

Eaten rolled his chaw in his lean jaws. "Dave Butler come over the Cut-Off with me, seen this ranch, then, an' nothin' would have it but that he come back here to settle. I reckon I know what he

wanted." He turned. "Doc, you'll git none of that
XY water today! Take this man to Ashton, then
put him in jail! An' make her fast!''

Doc was a lean, saturnine man with a lantern
jaw and cold eyes. He glanced at Gatlin, then
nodded, "If yuh say so, Sheriff. I sure was hopin'
for some o' that good XY water, though. Come
on, podner.''

They wheeled their horses and started for Tucker,
Doc turning from the trail to cross the desert through
a thick tangle of cedar and sage brush. "Mite
quicker this-away. Ain't nobody ever rides it, an'
she's some rough.''

It was high noon and the sun was blazing. Doc
led off, casting only an occasional glance back at
Gatlin. Jim was puzzled, for the man made no
show of guarding him. Was he deliberately offer-
ing him the chance to make a break? It looked it,
but Jim wasn't having any. His one idea was to get
to Tucker, see Ashton and get his money down.
They rode on, pushing through the dancing heat
waves, no breeze stirring the air, and the sun
turning the bowl into a baking oven.

Doc slowed the place a little. "Hosses won't
stand it,'' he commented, then glanced at Gatlin.
"I reckon you're honest. Yuh had a chance for a
break an' didn't take it.'' He grinned wryly. "Not
that yuh'd have got fur. This here ol' rifle o' mine
sure shoots where I aim it at.''

"I've nothin' to run from," Gatlin replied. "What

I've said was true. My bein' in Tucker was strictly accidental."

The next half mile they rode side by side, entering now into a devil's playground of boulders and arroyos. Doc's hand went out and Jim drew up. Buzzards roosted in a tree not far off the trail, a half dozen of the great birds. "Somethin' dead," Doc said. "Let's have a look."

Two hundred yards farther and they drew up. What had been a dappled gray horse lay in a saucer-like depression among the cedars. Buzzards lifted from it, flapping their great wings. Doc's eyes glinted and he spat. "Jim Walker's mare," he said, "an' his saddle."

They pushed on, circling the dead horse. Gatlin pointed. "Look," he said, "he wasn't killed. He was crawlin' away."

"Yeah," Doc was grim, "but not fur. Look at the blood he was losin'."

They got down from their horses, their faces grave. Both men knew what they'd find, and neither man was happy. Doc slid his rifle from the scabbard. "Jim Walker was by way o' bein' a friend o' mine," he said. "I take his goin' right hard."

The trail was easy. Twice the wounded man had obviously lain still for a long time. They found torn cloth where he had ripped up his shirt to bandage a wound. They walked on until they saw the gray rocks and the foot of the low bluff. It was a cul-de-sac.

"Wait a minute," Gatlin said. "Look at this." He indicated the tracks of a man who had walked up the trail. He had stopped here, and there was blood on the sage, spattered blood. The faces of the men hardened, for the deeper impression of one foot, the way the step was taken and the spattered blood told but one thing. The killer had walked up and kicked the wounded man!

They had little farther to go. The wounded man had nerve, and nothing had stopped him. He was backed up under a clump of brush that grew from the side of the bluff, and he lay on his face. That was an indication to these men that Walker had been conscious for some time, that he had sought a place where the buzzards couldn't get at him.

Doc turned, and his gray white eyes were icy. "Step your boot beside that track," he said, his rifle partly lifted.

Jim Gatlin stared back at the man and felt something cold and empty inside him. At that moment, familiar with danger as he was, he was glad he wasn't the killer. He stepped over to the tracks and made a print beside them. His boot was almost an inch shorter and of a different type.

"Didn't figger so," Doc said. "But I aimed to make sure."

"On the wall there," Gatlin said. "He scratched somethin'."

Both men bent over. It was plain, scratched with an edge of whitish rock on the slate of a small slab, *Cary done* . . . and no more.

Doc straightened. "He kin wait a few hours more. Let's git to town."

*   *   *

Tucker's street was more crowded than usual when they rode up to Ashton's office and swung down. Jim Gatlin pulled open the door and stepped in. The tall, gray-haired man behind the desk looked up. "You're Ashton?" Gatlin demanded.

At the answering nod, he opened his shirt and unbuckled his money belt. "There's ten thousand there. Bid in the XY for Cochrane an' Gatlin."

Ashton's eyes sparkled with sudden satisfaction. "You're her partner?" he asked. "You're putting up the money? It's a fine thing you're doing, man."

"I'm a partner only in name. My gun backs the brand, that's all. She may need a gun behind her for a little while, an' I've got it."

He turned to Doc, but the man was gone. Briefly, Gatlin explained what they had found, and added, "Wing Cary's headed for town now."

"Headed for town?" Ashton's head jerked around. "He's here. Came in about twenty minutes ago!"

Jim Gatlin spun on his heel and strode from the office. On the street, pulling his hat brim low against the glare, he stared left, then right. There were men on the street, but they were drifting inside now. There was no sign of the man called Doc or of Cary.

Gatlin's heels were sharp and hard on the boardwalk. He moved swiftly, his hands swinging alongside his guns. His hard brown face was cool and his lips were tight. At the Barrelhouse, he paused, put up his left hand and stepped in. All faces turned toward him, but none was that of Cary. "Seen Wing Cary?" he demanded. "He murdered Jim Walker."

Nobody replied, and then an oldish man turned his head and jerked it down the street. "He's gettin' his hair cut, right next to the livery barn. Waitin' fur the auction to start up."

Gatlin stepped back through the door. A dark figure, hunched near the blacksmith shop, jerked back from sight. Jim hesitated, alert to danger, then quickly pushed on.

The red-and-white barber pole marked the frame building. Jim opened the door and stepped in. A sleeping man snored with his mouth open, his back to the street wall. The bald barber looked up, swallowed and stepped back.

Wing Cary sat in the chair, his hair half trimmed, the white cloth draped around him. The opening door and sudden silence made him look up. "You, is it?" he said.

"It's me. We found Jim Walker. He marked your name, Cary, as his killer."

Cary's lips tightened and suddenly a gun bellowed and something slammed Jim Gatlin in the shoulder and spun him like a top, smashing him sidewise into the door. That first shot saved him from the second. Wing Cary had held a gun in his lap and fired through the white cloth. There was sneering triumph in his eyes, and as though time stood still Jim Gatlin saw the smoldering of the black-rimmed circles of the holes in the cloth.

He never remembered firing, but suddenly Cary's body jerked sharply, and Jim felt the gun buck in his hand. He fired again then, and Wing's face twisted and his gun went into the floor, narrowly missing his own foot.

Wing started to get up, and Gatlin fired the third time, the shot nicking Wing's ear and smashing a shaving cup, spattering lather. The barber was on his knees in one corner, holding a chair in front of him. The sleeping man had dived through the window, glass and all.

Men came running, and Jim leaned back against the door. One of the men was Doc, and he saw Sheriff Eaton, and then Lisa tore them aside and ran to him. "Oh, you're hurt! You've been shot! You've . . . !"

His feet gave away slowly and he slid down the door to the floor. Wing Cary still sat in the barber shop, his hair half clipped.

Doc stepped in and glanced at him, then at the barber. "Yuh can't charge him fur it, Tony. Yuh never finished!"

DESERT DEATH-
SONG

When Jim Morton rode up to the fire three un-shaven men huddled there warming themselves and drinking hot coffee. Morton recognized Chuck Benson from the Slash Five. The other men were strangers.

"Howdy, Chuck!" Morton said. "He still in there?"

"Sure is!" Benson told him. "An' it don't look like he's figurin' on comin' out."

"I don't reckon to blame him. Must be a hundred men scattered about."

"Nigher two hundred, but you know Nat Bodine. Shakin' him out of these hills is going to be tougher'n shaking a possum out of a tree."

The man with the black beard stubble looked up

sourly. "He wouldn't last long if they'd let us go in after him! I'd sure roust him out of there fast enough!"

Morton eyed the man with distaste. "You think so. That means you don't know Bodine. Goin' in after him is like sendin' a houn' dog down a hole after a badger. That man knows these hills, ever' crack an' crevice! He can hide places an Apache would pass up."

The black-bearded man stared sullenly. He had thick lips and small, heavy-lidded eyes. "Sounds like maybe you're a friend of his'n. Maybe when we get him you should hang alongside of him."

Somehow the long rifle over Morton's saddle bows shifted to stare warningly at the man, although Morton made no perceptible movement. "That ain't a handy way to talk, stranger," Morton said casually. "Ever'body in these hills knows Nat, an' most of us been right friendly with him one time or another. I ain't takin' up with him, but I reckon there's worse men in this posse than he is."

"Meanin'?" The big man's hand lay on his thigh.

"Meanin' anything you like." Morton was a Tennessee mountain man before he came west and gun talk was no strange to him. "You call it your ownself." The long rifle was pointed between the big man's eyes and Morton was building a cigarette with his hands only inches away from the trigger.

"Forget it!" Benson interrupted. "What you two got to fight about? Blackie, this here's Jim Morton. He's lion hunter for the Lazy S."

Blackie's mind underwent a rapid readjustment. This tall, lazy stranger wasn't the soft-headed drink of water he had thought him, for everybody knew about Morton. A dead shot with rifle and pistol, he was known to favor the former, even in fairly close combat. He had been known to go up trees after mountain lions and once, when three hardcase rustlers had tried to steal his horses, the three had ended up in Boothill.

"How about it, Jim?" Chuck asked. "You know Nat. Where'd you think he'd be?"

Morton squinted and drew on his cigarette. "Ain't no figurin' him. I know him, an' I've hunted along of him. He's almighty knowin' when it comes to wild country. Moves like a cat an' got eyes like a turkey buzzard." He glanced at Chuck. "What's he done? I heard some talk down to the Slash Five, but nobody seemed to have it clear."

"Stage robbed yestiddy. Pete Daley of the Diamond D was ridin' it, an' he swore the robber was Nat. When they went to arrest him, Nat shot the sheriff."

"Kill him?"

"No. But he's bad off, an' like to die. Nat only fired once an' the bullet took Larabee too high."

"Don't sound reasonable," Morton said slowly. "Nat ain't one to miss somethin' he aims to kill. You say Pete Daley was there?"

"Yeah. He's the on'y one saw it."

"How about this robber? Was he masked?"

"Uh huh, an' packin' a Winchester .44 an' two tied-down guns. Big black-headed man, the driver said. He didn't know Bodine, but Pete identified him."

Morton eyed Benson. "I shouldn't wonder," he said, and Chuck flushed.

Each knew what the other was thinking. Pete Daley had never liked Bodine. Nat married the girl Pete wanted, even though it was generally figured Pete never had a look-in with her, anyway, but Daley had worn his hatred like a badge ever since. Mary Callahan had been a pretty girl, but a quiet one, and Daley had been sure he'd win her.

But Bodine had come down from the hills and changed all that. He was a tall man with broad shoulders, dark hair and a quiet face. He was a good looking man, even a handsome man, some said. Men liked him, and women too, but the men liked him best because he left their women alone. That was more than could be said for Daly, who lacked Bodine's good looks but made up for it with money.

Bodine had bought a place near town and drilled a good well. He seemed to have money, and that puzzled people, so hints began to get around that he had been rustling as well as robbing stages. There were those, like Jim Morton who believed most of the stories stemmed from Daley, but no matter where they originated, they got around.

Hanging Bodine for killing the sheriff—the fact that he was still alive was overlooked, and considered merely a technical question, anyway—was the problem before the posse. It was a self elected posse, inspired to some extent by Daley, and given a semi official status by the presence of Burt Stoval, Larrabee's jailer.

Yet to hang a man he must first be caught and Bodine had lost himself in that broken, rugged country known as Powder Basin. It was a region of some ten square miles backed against an even rougher and uglier patch of waterless desert, but the basin was bad enough itself.

Fractured with gorges and humped with fir-clad hogbacks, it was a maze where the juniper region merged into the fir and spruce, and where the canyons were liberally overgrown with manzanita. There were at least two cliff dwellings in the area, and a ghost mining town of some dozen ramshackle structures, tumbled-in and wind-worried.

"All I can say," Morton said finally, "is that I don't envy those who corner him—when they do and if they do."

Blackie wanted no issue with Morton, yet he was still sore. He looked up. "What do you mean, if we do? We'll get him!"

Morton took his cigarette from his lips. "Want a suggestion, friend? When he's cornered, don't you be the one to go in after him."

*   *   *

Four hours later, when the sun was moving toward noon, the net had been drawn tighter, and Nat Bodine lay on his stomach in the sparse grass on the crest of a hogback and studied the terrain below.

There were many hiding places, but the last thing he wanted was to be cornered and forced to fight it out. Until the last moment he wanted freedom of movement.

Among the searchers were friends of his, men with whom he rode and hunted, men he had admired and liked. Now, they believed him wrong, they believed him a killer, and they were hunting him down.

They were searching the canyons with care, so he had chosen the last spot they would examine, a bald hill with only the foot high grass for cover. His vantage point was excellent, and he had watched with appreciation the care with which they searched the canyon below him.

Bodine scooped another handful of dust and rubbed it along his rifle barrel. He knew how far a glint of sunlight from a rifle barrel can be seen, and men in that posse were Indian fighters and hunters.

No matter how he considered it, his chances were slim. He was a better woodsman than any of them, unless it was Jim Morton. Yet that was not enough. He was going to need food and water.

Sooner or later they would get the bright idea of watching the waterholes, and after that. . . .

It was almost twenty-four hours since he had eaten, and he would soon have to refill his canteen.

Pete Daley was behind this, of course. Trust Pete not to tell the true story of what happened. Pete had accused him of the holdup right to his face when they had met him on the street. The accusation had been sudden, and Nat's reply had been prompt. He'd called Daley a liar, and Daley moved a hand for his gun. The sheriff sprang to stop them and took Nat's bullet. The people who rushed to the scene saw only the sheriff on the ground, Daley with no gun drawn, and Nat gripping his six-shooter. Yet it was not that of which he thought now. He thought of Mary.

What would she be thinking now? They had been married so short a time, and had been happy despite the fact that he was still learning how to live in civilization and with a woman. It was a mighty different thing, living with a girl like Mary.

Did she doubt him now? Would she, too, believe he had held up the stage and then killed the sheriff? As he lay in the grass he could find nothing on which to build hope.

Hemmed in on three sides, with the waterless mountains and desert behind him, the end seemed inevitable. Thoughtfully, he shook his canteen. It was nearly empty. Only a little water sloshed weakly in the bottom. Yet he must last the afternoon

through, and by night he could try the waterhole
at Mesquite Springs, no more than a half mile
away.

The sun was hot, and he lay very still, knowing
that only the faint breeze should stir the grass
where he lay if he were not to be seen.

Below him he heard men's voices, and from
time to time could distinguish a word or even
sentence. They were cursing the heat, but their
search was not relaxed. Twice men mounted the
hill and passed near him. One man stopped for
several minutes, not more than a dozen yards away,
but Nat held himself still and waited. Finally the
man moved on, mopping sweat from his face.
When the sun was gone he wormed his way off the
crest and into the manzanita. It took him over an
hour to get within striking distance of Mesquite
Springs. He stopped just in time. His nostrils caught
the faint fragrance of tobacco smoke.

Lying in the darkness, he listened, and after a
moment heard a stone rattle, then the faint *chink* of
metal on stone.

When he was far enough away he got to his feet
and worked his way through the night toward Stone
Cup, a spring two miles beyond. He moved more
warily now, knowing they were watching the
waterholes.

The stars were out, sharp and clear, when he
snaked his way through the reeds toward the cup.
Deliberately, he chose the route where the over-

flow from the Stone Cup kept the earth soggy and high-grown with reeds and dank grass. There would be no chance of a watcher waiting there on the wet ground, nor would the wet grass rustle. He moved close, but here, too, men waited.

He lay still in the darkness, listening. Soon he picked out three men, two back in the shadows of the rock shelf, one over under the brush but not more than four feet from the small pool's edge.

There was no chance to get a canteen filled here, for the watchers were too wide awake. Yet he might manage a drink.

He slid his knife from his pocket and opened it carefully. He cut several reeds, allowing no sound. When he had them cut, he joined them and reached them toward the water. Lying on his stomach within only a few feet of the pool, and no farther from the nearest watcher, he sucked on the reeds until the water started flowing. He drank for a long time, then drank again. The trickle doing little, at first to assuage his thrist. After a while he felt better.

He started to withdraw the reeds, then grinned and let them lay. With care he worked his way back from the cup and got to his feet. His shirt was muddy and wet, and with the wind against his body he felt almost cold. With the waterholes watched there would be no chance to fill his canteen, and the day would be blazing hot. There might be an unwatched hole, but the chance of that was slight and if he spent the night in fruitless search of water he would exhaust his strength and lose the sleep he needed. Returning like a deer, to a resting place near a ridge, he bedded down in a clump of manzanita. His rifle cradled in his arm, he was almost instantly asleep. . . .

Dawn was breaking when he awakened, and his nostrils caught a whiff of wood smoke. His pursuers were at their breakfasts. By now they would have found his reeds, and he grinned at the thought of their anger at having had him so near without knowing. Morton, he reflected, would appreciate that. Yet they would all know he was short of water.

Worming his way through the brush, he found a trail that followed just below the crest, and moved steadily along in the partial shade, angling toward a towering hogback.

Later, from well up on the hogback, he saw three horsemen walking their animals down the ridge where he had rested the previous day. Two more were working up a canyon, and wherever he looked they seemed to be closing in. He abandoned the canteen, for it banged against brush and could be heard too easily. He moved back, going from one cluster of boulders to another, then pausing short of the ridge itself.

The only route that lay open was behind him, into the desert, and that way they were sure he would not go. The hogback on which he lay was the highest ground in miles, and before him the jagged scars of three canyons running off the hogback stretched their ugly length into the rocky, brush blanketed terrain. Up those three canyons groups of searchers were working. Another group had cut down from the north and come between him and the desert ghost town.

The far-flung skirmishing line was well disposed, and Nat could find it in himself to admire their skill. These were his brand of men, and they understood their task. Knowing them as he did, he knew how relentless they could be. The country behind him was open. It would not be open long. Knowing themselves, they were sure he would fight it out rather than risk dying of thirst in the desert. They were wrong.

Nat Bodine learned that suddenly. Had he been asked, he would have accepted their solution, yet now he saw that he could not give up.

The desert was the true Powder Basin. The Indians had called it The Place of No Water, and he had explored deep into it in the past years, and found nothing. While the distance across was less than twenty miles, a man must travel twice that or more, up and down and around, if he would cross it, and his sense of direction must be perfect. Yet, with water and time a man might cross it. And Nat Bodine had neither. Moreover, if he went into the desert they would soon send word and have men waiting on the other side. He was fairly trapped, and yet he knew that he would die in that waste alone, before he'd surrendered to be lynched. Nor could he hope to fight off this posse for long.

Carefully he got to his feet and worked his way to
the maw of the desert. He nestled among the
boulders and watched the men below. They were
coming carefully, still several yards away. Cra-
dling his Winchester against his cheek, he drew a
bead on a rock ahead of the nearest man, and
fired.

Instantly the searchers vanished. Where a dozen
men had been in sight, there was nobody now. He
chuckled. "That made 'em eat dirt!" he said.
"Now they won't be so anxious."

The crossing of the crest was dangerous, but he
made it, and hesitated there, surveying the scene
before him. Far away to the horizon stretched the
desert. Before him the mountain broke sharply
away in a series of sheer precipices and ragged
chasms, and he scowled as he stared down at
them, for there seemed no descent could be possible from here.

*   *   *

Chuck Benson and Jim Morton crouched in the
lee of a stone wall and stared up at the ridge from
which the shot had come. "He didn't shoot to
kill," Morton said, "or he'd have had one of
us. He's that good."

"What's on his mind?" Benson demanded. "He's
stuck now. I know that ridge an' the only way
down is the way he went up."

"Let's move in," Blackie protested. "There's cover enough."

"You don't know Nat. He's never caught until you see him down. I know the man. He'll climb cliffs that would stop a hoss fly."

Pete Daley and Burt Stoval moved up to join them, peering at the ridge before them through the concealing leaves. The ridge was a gigantic hogback almost a thousand feet higher than the plateau on which they waited. On the far side it fell away to the desert, dropping almost two thousand feet in no more than two hundred yards, and most of the drop in broken cliffs.

Daley's eyes were hard with satisfaction. "We got him now!" he said triumphantly. "He'll never get off that ridge! We've only to wait a little, then move in on him. He's out of water, too!"

Mortion looked with distaste at Daley. "You seem powerful anxious to get him, Pete. Maybe the sheriff ain't dead yet. Maybe he won't die. Maybe his story of the shootin' will be different."

Daley turned on Morton, his dislike evident. "Your opinion's of no account, Morton. I was there, and I saw it. As for Larabee, if he ain't dead he soon will be. If you don't like this job, why don't you leave?"

Jim Morton stoked his pipe calmly. "Because I aim to be here if you get Bodine," he said, "an' I personally figure to see he gets a fair shake. Furthermore, Daley, I'm not beholdin' to you, no way, an' I ain't scared of you. Howsoever, I figure you've got a long way to go before you get Bodine.''

High on the ridge, flat on his stomach among the rocks, Bodine was not so sure. He mopped sweat from his brow and studied again the broken cliff beneath him. There seemed to be a vaguely possible route but at the thought of it his mouth turned dry and his stomach empty.

A certain bulge in the rock looked as though it might afford handholds, although some of the rock was loose, and he couldn't see below the bulge where it might become smooth. Once over that projection, getting back would be difficult if not impossible. Nevertheless, he determined to try.

Using his belt for a rifle strap, he slung the Winchester over his back, then turned his face to the rock and slid feet first over the bulge, feeling with his toes for a hold. If he fell from here, he could not drop less than two hundred feet, although close in there was a narrow ledge only sixty feet down.

Using simple pull holds, and working down with his feet, Bodine got well out over the bulge. Taking a good grip, he turned his head and searched the rock below him. On his left the rock was cracked deeply, with the portion of the face to which he clung projecting several inches farther into space than the other side of the crack. Shifting his left foot carefully, he stepped into the crack, which afforded a good jam hold. Shifting his left hand, he took a pull grip, pulling away from himself with the left fingers until he could swing his body to the left, and get a grip on the edge of the crack with his right fingers. Then lying back, his feet braced against the projecting far edge of the crack, and pulling toward himself with his hands, he worked his way down, step by step and grip by grip, for all of twenty feet. There the crack widened into a chimney, far too wide to be climbed with a lie back, its inner sides slick and smooth from the scouring action of wind and water.

Working his way into the chimney, he braced his feet against one wall and his back against the other, and by pushing against the two walls and shifting his feet carefully, he worked his way down until he was well past the sixty foot ledge. The chimney ended in a small cavern-like hollow in the rock, and he sat there, catching his breath.

Nat ran his fingers through his hair and mopped sweat from his brow. Anyway, he grinned at the thought, they wouldn't follow him down here!

Carefully, he studied the cliff below him, then to the right and left. To escape his present position he must make a traverse of the rock face, working his way gradually down. For all of forty feet of climb he would be exposed to a dangerous fall, or to a shot from above if they had dared the ridge. Yet there were precarious handholds and some inch-wide ledges for his feet.

When he had his breath, he moved out, clinging to the rock face and carefully working across it and down. Sliding down a steep slab, he crawled out on a knife edge ridge of rock and straddling it, worked his way along until he could climb down a further face, hand over hand. Landing on a wide ledge, he stood there, his chest heaving, staring back up at the ridge. No one was yet in sight, and there was a chance that he was making good his escape. At the same time his mouth was dry and the effort expended in climbing and descending had increased his thirst. Unslinging his rifle, he completed the descent without trouble, emerging at last upon the desert below.

Heat lifted against his face in a stifling wave. Loosening the buttons of his shirt, he pushed back his hat and stared up at the towering height of the mountain, and even as he looked up, he saw men appear on the ridge. Lifting his hat, he waved to them.

Benson was the first man on that ridge, and involuntarily he drew back from the edge of the cliff, catching his breath at the awful depth below. Pete Daley, Burt Stoval and Tim Morgan moved up beside him, and then the others. It was Morgan who spotted Bodine first.

"What did I tell you?" he snapped. "He's down there on the desert!"

Daley's face hardened. "Why, the dirty—"

Benson stared. "You got to hand it to him!" he said. "I'd sooner chance a shootout than try that cliff!"

A bearded man on their left spat and swore softly. "Well, boys, this does it! I'm quittin! No man that game deserves to hang! I'd say, let him go!"

Pete Daley turned angrily, but changed his mind when he saw the big man and the way he wore his gun. Pete was no fool. Some men could be bullied, and it was a wise man who knew which and when. "I'm not quitting," he said flatly. "Let's get the boys, Chuck. We'll get our horses and be around there in a couple of hours. He won't get far on foot."

*   *   *

Nat Bodine turned and started off into the desert with a long swinging stride. His skin felt hot, and the air was close and stifling, yet his only chance was to get across this stretch and work into the hills at a point where they could not find him.

All this time Mary was in the back of his mind, her presence always near, always alive. Where was she now? And what was she doing? Had she been told?

Nat Bodine had emerged upon the desert at the mouth of one of a boulder-strewn canyon slashed deep into the rocky flank of the mountain itself.

From the mouth of the canyon there extended a wide fan of rock, coarse gravel, sand and silt flushed down from the mountain by torrential rains. On his right the edge of the fan of sand was broken by the deep scar of another wash, cut at some later date when the water had found some crevice in the rock to give it an unexpected hold. It was toward this wash that Bodine walked.

Clambering down the slide, he walked along the bottom. Working his way among the boulders, he made his way toward the shimmering basin that marked the extreme low level of the desert. Here, dancing with heat waves, and seeming from a distance to be a vast blue lake, was one of those dry lakes that collect the muddy runoff from the mountains. Yet as he drew closer he discovered he had been mistaken in his hope that it was a *playa* of the dry type. Wells sunk in the dry type of *playa* often produce fresh cool water, and occasionally at shallow depths. This, however, was a pasty, water surfaced *salinas,* and water found here would be salty and worse than none at all. Moreover, there was danger that he might break through the crust beneath the dry powdery dust and into the slime below.

The *playa* was such that it demanded a wide detour from his path, and the heat here was even more intense than on the mountain. Walking steadily, dust rising at each footfall, Bodine turned left along the desert, skirting the *playa*. Beyond it he could see the edge of a rocky escarpment, and this rocky ledge stretched for miles toward the far mountain range bordering the desert.

Yet the escarpment must be attained as soon as possible, for knowing as he was in desert ways and lore, Nate understood in such terrain there was always a possibility of stumbling upon one of those desert tanks, or *tinajas,* which contain the purest water any wanderer of the dry lands could hope to find. Yet he knew how difficult these were to find, for hollowed by some sudden cascade, or scooped by wind, they are often filled to the brim with gravel or sand, and must be scooped out to obtain the water in the bottom.

Nat Bodine paused, shading his eyes toward the end of the *playa.* It was not much farther. His mouth was powder dry now, and he could swallow only with an effort.

He was no longer perspiring. He walked as in a daze, concerned only with escaping the basin of the *playa,* and it was with relief that he stumbled over a stone and fell headlong. Clumsily, he got to his feet, blinking away the dust and pushing on through the rocks. He crawled to the top of the escarpment through a deep crack in the rock and then walked on over the dark surface.

It was some ancient flow of lava, crumbling to ruin now, with here and there a broken blister of it. In each of them he searched for water, but they were dry. At this hour he would see no coyote, but he watched for tracks, knowing the wary and wily desert wolves knew where water could be found.

The horizon seemed no nearer, nor had the peaks begun to show their lines of age, or the shapes into which the wind had carved them. Yet the sun was lower now, its rays level and blasting as the searing flames of a furnace. Bodine plodded on, walking toward the night, hoping for it, praying for it. Once he paused abruptly at a thin whine of sound across the sun-blasted air.

Waiting, he listened, searching the air about him with eyes suddenly alert, but he did not hear the sound again for several minutes, and when he did hear it there was no mistaking it. His eyes caught the dark movement, striking straight away from him on a course diagonal with his own.

A bee!

Nat changed his course abruptly, choosing a landmark on a line with the course of the bee, and then followed on. Minutes later he saw a second bee, and altered his course to conform with it. The direction was almost the same, and he knew that water could be found by watching converging lines of bees. He could afford to miss no chance, and he noted the bees were flying deeper *into* the desert, not away from it.

Darkness found him suddenly. At the moment the horizon range had grown darker, its crest tinted with old rose and gold, slashed with the deep fire of crimson, and then it was night, and a coyote was yapping myriad calls at the stars.

In the coolness he might make many miles by pushing on, and he might also miss his only chance at water. He hesitated, then his weariness conformed with his judgment, and he slumped down against a boulder and dropped his chin on his chest. The coyote voiced a shrill complaint, then satisfied with the echo against the rocks, ceased his yapping and began to hunt. He scented the man smell and skirted wide around, going about his business.

*   *   *

There were six men in the little cavalcade at the base of the cliff, searching for tracks. The rider found them there. Jim Morton calmly sitting his horse and watching with interested eyes, but lending no aid to the men who tracked his friend, and there were Pete Daley, Blackie, Chuck Benson and Burt Stoval. Farther along were other groups of riders.

The man worked a hard-ridden horse and he was yelling before he reached them. He raced up and slid his horse to a stop, gasping, "Call it off! It wasn't him!"

"What?" Daley burst out. "What did you say?"

"I said . . . it wa'n't Bodine! We got our outlaw

this mornin' out east of town! Mary Bodine spotted a man hidin' in the brush below Wenzel's
place, an' she come down to town. It was him, all
right. He had the loot on him, an' the stage driver
identified him!''

Pete Daley stared, his little eyes tightening.
"What about the sheriff?" he demanded.

"He's pullin' through." The rider stared at Daley.
"He said it was his fault he got shot. His an'
your'n. He said if you'd kept your fool mouth shut
nothin' would have happened, an' that he was a
another fool for not lettin' you get leaded down like
you deserved!''

Daley's face flushed, and he looked around angrily like a man badly treated. "All right, Benson.
We'll go home."

"Wait a minute." Jim Morton crossed his hands
on the saddle horn. "What about Nat? He's out
there in the desert an' he thinks he's still a hunted
man. He's got no water. Far's we know, he may
be dead by now."

Daley's face was hard. "He'll make out. My time's
too valuable to chase around in the desert after a
no-account hunter."

"It wasn't too valuable when you had an excuse
to kill him," Morton said flatly.

"I'll ride with you, Morton," Benson offered.

Daley turned on him, his face dark. "You do
an' you'll hunt you a job!"

Benson spat. "I quit workin' for you ten minutes ago. I never did like coyotes."

He sat his horse, staring hard at Daley, waiting to see if he would draw, but the rancher merely stared back until his eyes fell. He turned his horse.

"If I were you," Morton suggested, "I'd sell out an' get out. This country don't cotton to your type, Pete."

Morton started his horse. "Who's comin'?"

"We all are." It was Blackie who spoke. "But we better fly some white. I don't want that salty Injun shootin' at me!"

It was near sundown of the second day of their search and the fourth since the holdup, that they found him. Benson had a shirt tied to his rifle barrel, and they took turns carrying it.

They had given up hope the day before, knowing he was out of water, and knowing the country he was in.

The cavalcade of riders were almost abreast of a shoulder of sandstone outcropping when a voice spoke out of the rocks. "You huntin' me?"

Jim Morton felt relief flood through him. "Huntin' you peaceful," he said. "They got their outlaw, an' Larrabee owes you no grudge."

His face burned red from the desert sun, his eyes squinting at them, Nat Bodine swung his long body down over the rocks. "Glad to hear that," he said. "I was some worried about Mary."

"She's all right." Morton stared at him. "What did you do for water?"

"Found some. Neatest *tinaja* in all this desert."

The men swung down and Benson almost stepped on a small, red spotted toad.

"Watch that, Chuck. That's the boy who saved my life."

"That toad?" Blackie was incredulous. "How d' you mean?"

"That kind of toad never gets far from water. You only find them near some permanent seepage or spring. I was all in, down on my hands and knees, when I heard him cheeping.

"It's a noise like a cricket, and I'd been hearing it sometime before I remembered that a Yaqui had told me about these frogs. I hunted, and found him, so I knew there had to be water close by. I'd followed the bees for a day and a half, always this way, and then I lost them. While I was studyin' the lay of the land, I saw another bee, an' then another. All headin' for this bunch of sand rock. But it was the toad that stopped me."

They had a horse for him, and he mounted up. Blackie stared at him. "You better thank that Morton," he said dryly. "He was the only one was sure you were in the clear."

"No, there was another," Morton said. "Mary was sure. She said you were no outlaw, and that you'd live. She said you'd live through anything." Morton bit off a chew, then glanced again at Nat. "They were wonderin' where you make your money, Nat."

"Me?" Bodine looked up, grinning. "Minin' turquoise. I found me a place where the Indians worked. I been cuttin' it out an' shippin' it east." He stooped and picked up the toad, and put him carefully in the saddlebag.

"That toad," he said emphatically, "goes home to Mary an' me. Our place is green an' mighty purty, an' right on the edge of the desert, but with plenty of water. This toad has got him a good home from here on, and I mean a good home!"

TRAP OF GOLD

Wetherton had been three months out of Horsehead before he found his first color. At first it was a few scattered grains taken from the base of an alluvial fan where millions of tons of sand and silt had washed down from a chain of rugged peaks; yet the gold was ragged under the magnifying glass.

Gold that has carried any distance becomes worn and polished by the abrasive action of the accompanying rocks and sand, so this could not have been carried far. With caution born of harsh experience he seated himself and lighted his pipe, yet excitement was strong within him.

A contemplative man by nature, experience had taught him how a man may be deluded by hope, yet all his instincts told him the source of the gold was somewhere on the mountain above. It could have come down the wash that skirted the base of the mountain, but the ragged condition of the gold made that improbable.

The base of the fan was a half-mile across and hundreds of feet thick, built of silt and sand washed down by centuries of erosion among the higher peaks. The point of the wide V of the fan lay between two towering upthrusts of granite, but from where Wetherton sat he could see that the actual source of the fan lay much higher.

Wetherton made camp near a tiny spring west of the fan, then picketed his burros and began his climb. When he was well over two thousand feet higher he stopped, resting again, and while resting he dry-panned some of the silt. Surprisingly, there were more than a few grains of gold even in that first pan, so he continued his climb, and passed at last between the towering portals of the granite columns.

Above this natural gate were three smaller alluvial fans that joined at the gate to pour into the greater fan below. Dry-panning two of these brought no results, but the third, even by the relatively poor method of dry-panning, showed a dozen colors, all of good size.

The head of this fan lay in a gigantic crack in a granite upthrust that resembled a fantastic ruin. Pausing to catch his breath, his gaze wandered along the base of this upthrust, and right before him the crumbling granite was slashed with a vein of quartz that was liberally laced with gold!

Struggling nearer through the loose sand, his heart pounding more from excitement than from altitude and exertion, he came to an abrupt stop. The band of quartz was six feet wide and that six feet was cobwebbed with gold.

It was unbelievable, but here it was.

Yet even in this moment of success, something about the beetling cliff stopped him from going forward. His innate caution took hold and he drew back to examine it at greater length. Wary of what he saw, he circled the batholith and then climbed to the ridge behind it from which he could look down upon the roof. What he saw from there left him dry-mouth and jittery.

The grantic batholith was obviously a part of a much older range, one that had weathered and worn, suffered from shock and twisting until finally this tower of granite had been violently upthrust, leaving it standing, a shaky ruin among younger and sturdier peaks. In the process the rock had been shattered and riven by mighty forces until it had become a miner's horror. Wetherton stared, fascinated by the prospect. With enormous wealth here for the taking, every ounce must be taken at the risk of life.

One stick of powder might bring the whole crumbling mass down in a heap, and it loomed all of three hundred feet above its base in the fan. The roof of the batholith was riven with gigantic cracks, literally seamed with breaks like the wall of an ancient building that has remained standing after heavy bombing. Walking back to the base of the tower. Wetherton found he could actually break loose chunks of the quartz with his fingers.

The vein itself lay on the downhill side and at the very base. The outer wall of the upthrust was sharply tilted so that a man working at the vein would be cutting his way into the very foundations of the tower, and any single blow of the pick might bring the whole mass down upon him. Furthermore, if the rock did fall, the vein would be hopelessly buried under thousands of tons of rock and lost without the expenditure of much more capital than he could command. And at this moment Wetherton's total of money in hand amounted to slightly less than forty dollars.

Thirty yards from the face he seated himself upon the sand and filled his pipe once more. A man might take tons out of there without trouble, and yet it might collapse at the first blow. Yet he knew he had no choice. He needed money and it lay here before him. Even if he were at first successful there were two things he must avoid. The first was tolerance of danger that might bring carelessness; the second, that urge to go back for that 'little bit more' that could kill him.

It was well into the afternoon and he had not eaten, yet he was not hungry. He circled the batholith, studying it from every angle only to reach the conclusion that his first estimate had been correct. The only way to get to the gold was to go into the very shadow of the leaning wall and attack it at its base, digging it out by main strength. From where he stood it seemed ridiculous that a mere man with a pick could topple that mass of rock, yet he knew how delicate such a balance could be.

The batholith was situated on what might be described as the military crest of the ridge, and the alluvial fan sloped steeply away from its lower side, steeper than a steep stairway. The top of the leaning wall over-shadowed the top of the fan, and if it started to crumble and a man had warning, he might run to the north with a bare chance of escape. The soft sand in which he must run would be an impediment, but that could be alleviated by making a walk from flat rocks sunken into the sand.

It was dark when he returned to his camp. Deliberately, he had not permitted himself to begin work, not by so much as a sample. He must be deliberate in all his actions, and never for a second should he forget the mass that towered above him. A split second of hesitation when the crash came— and he accepted it as inevitable—would mean burial under tons of crumbled rock.

The following morning he picketed his burros on a small meadow near the spring, cleaned the spring itself and prepared a lunch. Then he removed his shirt, drew on a pair of gloves and walked to the face of the cliff. Yet even then he did not begin, knowing that upon this habit of care and deliberation might depend not only his success in the venture, but life itself. He gathered flat stones and began building his walk. "When you start moving," he told himself, "you'll have to be fast."

Finally, and with infinite care, he began tapping at the quartz, enlarging cracks with the pick, removing fragments, then prying loose whole chunks. He did not swing the pick, but used it as a lever. The quartz was rotten, and a man might obtain a considerable amount by this method of picking or even pulling with the hands. When he had a sack filled with the richest quartz he carried it over his path to a safe place beyond the shadow of the tower. Returning, he tamped a few more flat rocks into his path, and began on the second sack. He worked with greater care than was, perhaps, essential. He was not and had never been a gambling man.

In the present operation he was taking a carefully calculated risk in which every eventuality had been weighed and judged. He needed the money and he intended to have it; he had a good idea of his chances of success, but knew that his gravest danger was to become too greedy, too much engrossed in his task.

Dragging the two sacks down the hill, he found a flat block of stone and with a single jack pro-

ceeded to break up the quartz. It was a slow and a
hard job but he had no better means of extracting
the gold. After breaking or crushing the quartz
much of the gold could be separated by a knife
blade, for it was amazingly concentrated. With
water from the spring Wetherton panned the re-
mainder until it was too dark to see.

Out of his blankets by daybreak he ate breakfast
and completed the extraction of the gold. At a
rough estimate his first day's work would run
to four hundred dollars. He made a cache for the
gold sack and took the now empty ore sacks and
climbed back to the tower.

The air was clear and fresh, the sun warm after
the chill of night, and he liked the feel of the pick
in his hands.

Laura and Tommy awaited him back in Horsehead, and if he was killed here, there was small
chance they would ever know what had become of
him. But he did not intend to be killed. The gold
he was extracting from this rock was for them, and
not for himself.

It would mean an easier life in a larger town, a
home of their own and the things to make the
home a woman desires, and it meant an education
for Tommy. For himself, all he needed was the
thought of that home to return to, his wife and
son—and the desert itself. And one was as necessary to him as the other.

The desert could be the death of him. He had
been told that many times, and did not need to be

told, for few men knew the desert as he did. The desert was to him what an orchestra is to a fine conductor, what the human body is to a surgeon. It was his work, his life, and the thing he knew best. He always smiled when he looked first into the desert as he started a new trip. Would this be it?

The morning drew on and he continued to work with an even-paced swing of the pick, a careful filling of the sack. The gold showed bright and beautiful in the crystalline quartz which was so much more beautiful than the gold itself. From time to time as the morning drew on, he paused to rest and to breathe deeply of the fresh, clear air. Deliberately, he refused to hurry.

For nineteen days he worked tirelessly, eight hours at day at first, then lessening his hours to seven, and then to six Wetherton did not explain to himself why he did this, but he realized it was becoming increasingly difficult to stay on the job. Again and again he would walk away from the rock face on one excuse or another, and each time he would begin to feel his scalp prickle, his steps grow quicker, and each time he returned more reluctantly.

Three times, beginning on the thirteenth, again on the seventeenth and finally on the nineteenth day, he heard movement within the tower. Whether that whispering in the rock was normal he did not know. Such a natural movement might have been going on for centuries. He only knew that it happened now, and each time it happened a cold chill went along his spine.

His work had cut a deep notch at the base of the tower, such a notch as a man might make in felling a tree, but wider and deeper. The sacks of gold, too, were increasing. They now numbered seven, and their total would, he believed, amount to more than five thousand dollars—probably nearer to six thousand. As he cut deeper into the rock the vein was growing richer.

He worked on his knees now. The vein had slanted downward as he cut into the base of the tower and he was all of nine feet into the rock with the great mass of it above him. If that rock gave way while he was working he would be crushed in an instant with no chance of escape. Nevertheless, he continued.

The change in the rock tower was not the only change, for he had lost weight and he no longer slept well. On the night of the twentieth day he decided he had six thousand dollars and his goal would be ten thousand. And the following day the rock was the richest ever! As if to tantalize him into working on and on, the deeper he cut the richer the ore became. By nightfall of that day he had taken out more than a thousand dollars.

Now the lust of the gold was getting into him, taking him by the throat. He was fascinated by the danger of the tower as well as the desire for the gold. Three more days to go—could he leave it then? He looked again at the batholith and felt a peculiar sense of foreboding, a feeling that here he was to die, that he would never escape. Was it his imagination, or had the outer wall leaned a little more?

On the morning of the twenty-second day he climbed the fan over a path that use had built into a series of continuous steps. He had never counted those steps but there must have been over a thousand of them. Dropping his canteen into a shaded hollow and pick in hand, he started for the tower.

The forward tilt *did* seem somewhat more than before. Or was it the light? The crack that ran behind the outer wall seemed to have widened and when he examined it more closely he found a small pile of freshly run silt near the bottom of the crack. So it had moved!

Wetherton hesitated, staring at the rock with wary attention. He was a fool to go back in there again. Seven thousand dollars was more than he had ever had in his life before, yet in the next few hours he could take out at least a thousand dollars more and in the next three days he could easily have the ten thousand he had set for his goal.

He walked to the opening, dropped to his knees and crawled into the narrowing, flat-roofed hole. No sooner was he inside than fear climbed up into his throat. He felt trapped, stifled, but he fought down the mounting panic and began to work. His first blows were so frightened and feeble that nothing came loose. Yet, when he did get started, he began to work with a feverish intensity that was wholly unlike him.

When he slowed and then stopped to fill his sack he was gasping for breath, but despite his hurry the sack was not quite full. Reluctantly, he lifted his pick again, but before he could strike a blow, the gigantic mass above him seemed to creak like something tired and old. A deep shudder went through the colossal pile and then a deep grinding that turned him sick with horror. All his plans for instant flight were frozen and it was not until the groaning ceased that he realized he was lying on his back, breathless with fear and expectancy. Slowly, he edged his way into the air and walked, fighting the desire to run, away from the rock.

When he stopped near his canteen he was wringing with cold sweat and trembling in every muscle. He sat down on the rock and fought for control. It was until some twenty minutes had passed that he could trust himself to get to his feet.

Despite his experience, he knew that if he did not go back now he would never go. He had out but one sack for the day and wanted another. Circling the batholith, he examined the widening crack, endeavoring again, for the third time, to find another means of access to the vein.

The tilt of the outer wall was obvious, and it could stand no more without toppling. It was possible that by cutting into the wall of the column and striking down he might tap the vein at a safer point. Yet this added blow at the foundation would bring the tower nearer to collapse and render his other hole untenable. Even this new attempt would not be safe, although immeasurably more secure than the hole he had left. Hesitating, he looked back at the hole.

Once more? The ore was now fabulously rich, and the few pounds he needed to complete the sack he could get in just a little while. He stared at the black and undoubtedly narrower hole, then looked up at the leaning wall. He picked up his pick and, his mouth dry, started back, drawn by a fascination that was beyond all reason.

His heart pounding, he dropped to his knees at the tunnel face. The air seemed stifling and he could feel his scalp tingling, but once he started to crawl it was better. The face where he now worked was at least sixteen feet from the tunnel mouth. Pick in hand, he began to wedge chunks from their seat. The going seemed harder now and the chunks did not come loose so easily. Above him the tower made no sound. The crushing weight was now something tangible. He could almost feel it growing, increasing with every move of his. The mountain seemed resting on his shoulder, crushing the air from his lungs.

Suddenly he stopped. His sack almost full, he stopped and lay very still, staring up at the bulk of the rock above him.

No.

He would go no further. Now he would quit. Not another sackful. Not another pound. He would go out now. He would go down the mountain without a backward look, and he would keep going. His wife waiting at home, little Tommy, who would run gladly to meet him—these were too much to gamble.

With the decision came peace, came certainty. He sighed deeply, and relaxed, and then it seemed to him that every muscle in his body had been knotted with strain. He turned on his side and with great deliberation gathered his lantern, his sack, his hand-pick.

He had won. He had defeated the crumbling tower, he had defeated his own greed. He backed easily, without the caution that had marked his earlier movements in the cave. His blind, trusting foot found the projecting rock, a piece of quartz that stuck out from the rough-hewn wall.

The blow was too weak, too feeble to have brought forth the reaction that followed. The rock seemed to quiver like the flesh of a beast when stabbed; a queer vibration went through that ancient rock, then a deep, gasping sigh.

He had waited too long!

Fear came swiftly in upon him, crowding him, while his body twisted, contracting into the smallest possible space. He tried to will his muscles to move beneath the growing sounds that vibrated through the passage. The whispers of the rock grew into a terrifying groan, and there was a rattle of pebbles. Then silence.

The silence was more horrifying than the sound. Somehow he was crawling, even as he expected the avalanche of gold to bury him. Abruptly, his feet were in the open. He was out.

He ran without stopping, but behind him he heard a growing roar that he couldn't outrace. When he knew from the slope of the land that he must be safe from falling rock, he fell to his knees. He turned and looked back. The muted, roaring sound, like thunder beyond mountains, continued, but there was no visible change in the batholith. Suddenly, as he watched, the whole rock formation seemed to shift and tip. The movement lasted only seconds, but before the tons of rock had found their new equilibrium, his tunnel and the area around it had utterly vanished from sight.

When he could finally stand. Wetherton gathered up his sack of ore and his canteen. The wind was cool upon his face as he walked away; and he did not look back again.